A SILENT ACCORD

The Clandestine Sapphire Society
Book 1

Kathy L Wheeler

ARE YOU SIGNED UP FOR DRAGONBLADE'S BLOG?

You'll get the latest news and information on exclusive giveaways, exclusive excerpts, coming releases, sales, free books, cover reveals and more.

Check out our complete list of authors, too!

No spam, no junk. That's a promise!

Sign Up Here

www.dragonbladepublishing.com

Dearest Reader;

Thank you for your support of a small press. At Dragonblade Publishing, we strive to bring you the highest quality Historical Romance from some of the best authors in the business. Without your support, there is no 'us', so we sincerely hope you adore these stories and find some new favorite authors along the way.

Happy Reading!

CEO, Dragonblade Publishing

❖⎯⎯⎯⎯◆⎯⎯⎯⎯❖

CHAPTER ONE

London 1827

Miss Verda Fairclough, sole child of the prestigious Right and Honorable Baron Krupt, paced the thick rug beneath frayed-silk-shod feet while she attempted to hold on to a fragile temper. Hers. "And just why am I learning this now?"

The baron hemmed and hawed about until Verda pointedly cleared her throat. "Er, well, I… It… You see…"

Her fists planted on slim hips, her foot tapped unsatisfyingly light against the rug. "Papa, I shall perish of old age. Get to it, if you please."

As was his usual reaction when backed against the proverbial wall, his shoulders drew up in a defensive tact like that of a cornered rat for attack. "It wasn't my fault."

Her arms fell to her sides, her hands squeezed into tight fists. She snapped her jaws shut and said through clenched teeth, "So, the dealer *shoved* the cards into your hand, *squeezed* your fingers until the coins to which you clung *clunked* to the table. Is that what you are trying to tell me?"

"Don't be insolent, Verda. No one at the table had coins." He let out an indignant sniff. "I am a gentleman and bound by my word."

She drew in a deep breath that did nothing to calm her unraveling nerves. "What of your duty to me, Papa? Am I worth so

1

little to you?"

With a defeated sigh, he pulled a white handkerchief from his pocket and dabbed it along his balding pate. "Of course not." He fell back into his chair behind a lavish but dusty and cluttered cherrywood desk. "The fact of the matter is our coffers are nearly dry. Those little ribbons and miniatures you paint for pin money…" He shook his head. "Pitiful."

Verda narrowed her eyes on her father. "Coffers dry? How nearly?" She was determined not to be taken in once again by the guileless innocence he'd always been able to project at will.

"If you don't marry a, er, gentleman of means, I fear we are bound for debtors' prison."

A long exhale deflated Verda's chest. "Truly?"

His response was a sharp nod. He was not jesting, then.

That was indeed serious. "I'm nine and twenty, Papa. I have no suitors." She dropped into the chair across from her father. "What do you propose I do? Get caught with a sagging bodice or expose my pantaloons at Peachornsby's grand ball Friday next?"

Papa stopped and gaped at her. An amusing sight had he not appeared so despondent. He managed a scowl. "Really, Verda. Must you be so explicit? I had another idea entirely. It requires your acquainting yourself with the Duke of Rathbourne."

"Rathbourne! He has a horrid reputation, Papa," she sputtered out.

He went on as if she hadn't spoken. "You'll wear your brightest and most fashionable frock. None of that brown and gray stuff you seem to favor. And, if that doesn't work…" He shrugged. "Then, well… we shall have to pack for Fleet."

As if one *could* pack for gaol, she thought grimly, shuddering at the same time. Nor would she be forced into the workhouse for her father's irresponsible tomfoolery.

"If you end up in Fleet, Papa, you shall have to manage alone, for I shall not be going with you. Nor will I visit," she said assured him tightly.

Never would she allow herself subjected to a dank, dark cell that would confine her as if in a grave or, worse, trapped with a dead body. Not again.

She would soon as dive off the cliffs of Dover first.

CHAPTER TWO

Three weeks later

RAIN SLASHED THE plush Pender carriage with a harsh wind carrying a frosty chill that went bone deep.

With his arms folded across his chest, Lysander Oshea leaned against the velvet squab while he considered his older brother, the Earl of Pender. At the best of times, Damien Oshea's actions could be rash and unpredictable. Other times, he was the jocund and loving brother Sander recalled from their youth. One just never knew from one moment to the next. "What the devil is wrong with you? I've never seen you like this. Perhaps you require a visit with your mistress and a thrashing beneath the sheets."

The low lantern light reflected Damien's straight, white teeth in a harsh grin. "Where the hell do you think I've been all night?" The smile of triumph transformed to a scowl. "Her scoundrel of a husband returned from sea less than an hour ago and I had to go out the window. Me! The Earl of Pender ducking out like a common housebreaker."

"Ah." That explained his restlessness. "So the man hadn't brandished a firearm?"

"Bugger off, Sander."

Sander narrowed his eyes, noting the tense brackets framing Damien's mouth, his stiffened jaw, the white-knuckled fists squeezed atop his thighs.

He flexed his fingers. "I've heard enough. Feel free to join me or languish out here in this miserable weather. Makes no difference to me."

The conveyance shook with the footman's descent from the box, but Damien kicked the door with a booted foot before the man could open it and jumped down where a puddle of muddied water marred his shiny Hessians.

Sander glanced out the carriage window to a wooden sign over the doors. *The Lyon's Den.* The breath left him in a rushed exhale. The place had a reputation unequaled to other hells. "What the devil?" he growled under his breath.

"I'm here to play the tables. My luck is changing. I can feel it," Damien shouted over the horrid weather.

Sander swallowed a groan. His option was to follow his brother and attempt to mitigate any damage incurred, as there would be no getting through to Damien now. He hurried out of the carriage. "Wait for me, Damien. I'm coming."

Inside a plush, dark lobby, they doffed their coats and hats to the arm of an efficient butler.

"Lord Pender, how lovely of you to join us this evening." The low lighting presented a lovely woman of an indeterminate age greeting them. She leaned around Damien and pierced Sander with a sharp gaze and a practiced smile. "Won't you introduce me to your guest, my lord?"

"Lysander Oshea, may I present the Black Widow of White-hall, Mrs. Dove-Lyon. Madam, my brother, Mr. Oshea."

She inclined her head. "How lovely to meet you, Mr. Oshea." She turned back to Damien. "I have just the table for you tonight. They've been awaiting the perfect partner. If you'll follow me, my lord."

Sander trailed his brother and Mrs. Dove-Lyon through a path that opened up as they made their way through a horde of men *and* women dressed as if for an exclusive ball. Only this wasn't a ballroom, nor was it the *ton*, though Sander recognized some of the more scandalous members. The Lyon's Den was one of the most notorious gaming hells London had to offer.

Despite his objections to the place, curiosity ate at Sander. The ambience of the den portrayed a decadence that bordered the absurd. Cushioned chairs covered in rich velvet. Walls draped with silk paper, Aubusson and Persian rugs on the floors leaving not an inch of wood exposed. Woven tapestries on the walls kept out the chilling winter night.

The most shocking sight was the presence of those women.

The Lady of Whitehall led them to a set of double doors, where a man almost as large as Sander threw them wide and ushered them in.

AN HOUR LATER, Sander was flexing his fingers then tightening them into fists at his back, having retreated from the table when the stakes had grown too uncomfortable. For him at least. Sander considered himself a sensible man. One who took few risks—*for very good reason.*

Not for Damien, however. His brother never worried over such mundane things like the fate of the Pender title and fortune.

The noise in the Den grew deafening, but Sander wasn't sure if it came from the contiguous conversation bounding off the paneled walls or the blood pounding through his veins to his ears. Several witnesses hovered over Damien now signing a vowel like vultures circling a dead corpse.

The pen swept over the paper in a theatrical flourish as if he had no other care in the world.

Sander didn't have to see his brother's expression to know he was seething with fury. It was there in the tension stretched across the back of his neck and shoulders.

Damien dropped the quill and shoved away from the table. "I need a drink," he snapped, stalking by Sander.

His brother's temper didn't come close to Sander's own. "You fool," he hissed. "What is it you hope to leave your sons after that preposterous exhibition?"

Damien didn't slow. "I can take care of my family."

Sander drew in a harsh breath and lowered his voice. "You just signed a contract forcing your heir to marry so you wouldn't lose the Cornwall property."

"What of it?"

Red hazed Sander's vision. "What of it? *What of it?* He's thirteen years old, for God's sake. You've just stolen his future from him."

"Don't be so dramatic. Rathbourne will be dead within a year. You mark my words."

"Rath—by whose edict? Yours? Are you planning murder now?"

"It's not a horrible idea." An indifferent shrug and a sneer indicated the sheer depths into which his brother had sunk.

Sander, built considerably larger than Damien's more slender elegance, folded his arms over his chest to keep from throttling him. "It is exactly a horrible idea," he said, grabbing his elder by the arm before he could slip away. He dragged him to a secluded corner. "At the very least, you'll be transported."

"Then you can take over the title. I'm fucking tired of it."

"You're spouting dribble, *Lord Pender*. You. Have. An. Heir. Even if I wished it, which I don't, Lucius is next in line, then Noah." Sander breathed in deeply, attempting to remain rational. One of them had to. "What of Lucius?" He gentled his tone. "Have you really thought of him and Noah? These are your children."

"Bah. We survived our own childhood, didn't we? They will as well." He leaned back and sneered, using the thick coat of cynicism he wielded so expertly, curling one lip in derision.

"Yes, but I seem to remember the two of us making a promise to one another not to treat our offspring as heartlessly as our sire treated us." *You*, he corrected silently.

"Perhaps it couldn't be helped," Damien said, his voice low

and barely discernable with the rising chatter about them.

Sander pinched the bridge of his nose. "You aren't making the slightest bit of sense. How can I help if I don't know the problem?"

"There is no problem," he bit out. "Now sod off."

"Damien…"

"I mean it, Sander. Leave me be." Damien strode off, back in the direction of an elaborate bar, leaving Sander at a loss. He and his brother had been quite close until almost two decades ago. Sander had been sixteen, Damien seventeen. Events around the time the devil himself—their father—had gone missing on the moors and was found dead the next day frozen through. A fitting end, if anyone cared to ask.

"Truly, Your Grace, I'm quite well. I can manage." The bold bark with its sultry undertone snapped Sander's attention away from the threat of darkness that always hovered, just beyond, always ready to suck him into the vortex. "Um, would you mind stepping back? I feel as if I can't breathe."

Sander's gaze swept past the crowd in the direction from which the words sounded, landing on a tall woman with hair as bright as a blood-red sun of a foreign horizon sinking into the ocean. It literally lighted the room. He might not have seen her cornered against the wall by that libertine the Duke of Rathbourne himself but for that mass of brilliance. His eyes drifted over her scarlet, lowcut gown edged in a delicate lace he'd bet his last farthing was Belgium. The gown's rich hue, up close, appeared more muted by the low, subtle lighting of the sconces.

"So, I leave you breathless as well, love." The duke's laugh was as low as his gaze on her bosom—all seduction and vastly inattentive, if the lady's expression was anything to go by.

Her eyes flashed fury? Panic? A chin that tilted just such. And a fist prepared to fly right into the duke's patrician nose.

Without an ounce of hesitation, Sander found himself sauntering toward them. "There you are, darling. I've been searching everywhere. I thought we were to meet in the supper room."

He met her startled gaze. Green. Brilliant emerald, green eyes. Their depths that matched the Pender jewels his mother used to wear that had long sense disappeared. The lady made a concerted effort to loosen her fingers and Sander slipped around Rathbourne and deftly retrieved this damsel gently by the arm.

She bristled beneath his touch but withheld comment.

Rathbourne grabbed her other arm, halting Sander's efforts to whisk her away. "What the hell are you about, Oshea? This is a private conversation. Find your own piece."

The lady's posture stiffened. "Piece?" she squeezed out through clenched teeth. "Did you just refer to me as a 'piece,' Your Grace?"

It looked as if her jaw were about to crack.

"Your father led me to believe you were available to… marry?" The duke seemed to choke on the last word.

"He was mistaken." She shot Sander a quick, unreadable glance.

Rathbourne's eyes narrowed over her willowy frame. "He said you would make an admirable replacement for my late wife. An adequate mother to my daughter, Meredith, for a small price."

Her finely shaped brows disappeared under a cask of curls lining her forehead. "Adequate? Small price?" Her eyes closed then opened, cast down over gloved hands, smoothing the silk of red skirts that should have clashed with her flaming hair but somehow didn't. "As I said, that is untrue"—she lifted her gaze, facing the duke squarely, defiantly—"as I am already wed."

Sander's entire insides went cold then hot. It was impossible to verify her statement with her fingers hidden within her gloves—red gloves—while she turned to him with a smile that could only be described as… cunning. The emerald eyes framed by thick, dark lashes blinked at him.

The chatter in the Den descended to a deafening and dramatic silence worthy of a Mozart opus.

Surely, she hadn't meant… but damn if he couldn't get the image of that flaming hair spread across his pillows.

Sander cleared his throat. "She is quite correct, Your Grace." Each uttered word gained him more confidence, though every muscle in his body was strung as taut as his favorite hunting bow. "If you ever refer to Mrs. Oshea—Mrs. *Lysander* Oshea"—God knew he had to get his name in there somehow—"as a 'piece' or anything close to such, there *will* be a dawn meeting. Remove your hand, Rathbourne." He would never know how he'd kept his voice so remarkably steady when the urge to wrap them about the duke's scrawny neck all but begged for action.

The duke's fingers opened as if burned by the heat of her body. He was not a large man. In fact, the duke was slight in build with deep-set eyes placed too close together between a long, pointed nose. The only thing going for the man were his deep pockets.

Deep pockets. Sander cast his "wife" another glance. Her expression remained inscrutable, but that was to be expected, he supposed. He knew her as well as she knew him. Which meant not at all.

Sander turned his back on Rathbourne and led her away, only to plow into another, more problematic obstacle. One not so easy to threaten.

"Married, Lysander?" Damien took her hand, which Rathbourne had abandoned. "'Tis news to me, brother," he murmured, brushing his lips over her gloved knuckles. He straightened and raked a practiced gaze over the lady in question that set Sander's blood afire even as the weight and stare of the crowd about them pierced him with thousands of tiny sharp pricks.

Sander couldn't imagine how the lady next to him felt. He went to shift her out of Damien's reach, but to Sander's surprise, she leaned into his arm, and damn if he couldn't feel the lush heat of her breasts through his coat.

"Can't you?" Her voice was sweet, demure, showing nothing of the boldness with which she'd hit Rathbourne. She turned such a guileless, innocent look on Sander, he thought his insides might ooze through the pores of his skin. "You didn't tell your brother?" She lightly tapped his arm with her fan and gave him a quick smile. "How perfectly horrid of you."

"Well played, madam," Damien said with a smile that set Sander's teeth on edge. He shot Sander a narrowed look that hinted at the mischievousness of their youth. He turned and ambled his way to a well-renowned courtesan who lifted a practiced brow and smile in his direction. "Until later."

CHAPTER THREE

EVERY WORD SPOUTING from Verda's mouth was another shovel of dirt burying her in a grave of her own making. She appreciated Mr. Oshea's attempt in shielding her from the Earl of Pender. She recognized the earl, of course. The bounder. His reputation was nearly as renowned as Rathbourne's. He'd made one advance on her years ago and she'd avoided him since.

First, and foremost, it was widely known Lord Pender was married, had his heir and his spare, with another child on the way. The man had no interest in her for the marriage Papa was pushing her toward.

Sadly, the duke's description of her as a woman who'd one day be an adequate mother seemed apt enough. She *would* make an apt wife. An apt mother. An apt anything, truth be told. Apt. She'd certainly been an apt caretaker for her mother until her death. If Papa ended up in gaol, somehow she'd have to find a way to survive.

Ha, she might make an *apt* whore. A burst of short laughter erupted from her, effectively startling her back to her present situation.

The unknown calculation in this quandary was her "supposed husband." They'd never met, as far as she could recall. He was tall, and broad. From the corner of her eye, she considered his etched, harsh features. But for the full lower lip that took her by surprise and left her fingers tingling for wont of smoothing away grooves that bracketed his mouth.

The sun-kissed face despite England's wintry January weather showed a man who spent a great deal of time in the outdoors. Perhaps he traveled by sea. Or farmed land.

With an internal shake of her head, she tamped back her curiosity. A second son? No, Mr. Lysander Oshea was not for the likes of her. With a coveted glance, she considered the throng about them as the hum of conversation picked up its normal whirr.

"Er, what shall we do now?" she muttered under her breath. Mostly to herself.

He leaned in, setting a more widespread prickle over her entire body. "Might I propose a run to Gretna Green?"

Verda's head snapped up, smacking his chin, or nose, or something, jarring hair from her sophisticated coiffure, which her maid had painstakingly affected. She shoved the unruly strands from her face. "What?" she said, keeping her voice low. A whisper, really, as the word was stuck in her throat. "You cannot be serious."

He rubbed his chin. "Why not?" His frown deepened the brackets. "You aren't truly married already, are you?"

Why not? Verda pulled up and dropped his arm she hadn't realized she was still holding. "Um, er, Mr. Oshea, I do appreciate your assistance with Rathbourne." She couldn't suppress the shudder. "I believe it's time I took my leave." She spun about and hurried away, feeling the ping of every eye in the place stabbing her between the shoulders.

A SENSE OF excitement pumped Sander's veins. The exquisite woman rushed from the large hall. He hadn't felt this alive since before his father's untimely demise. She was lovely in a way he wouldn't mind waking next to every morning. A small smile touched him. He started to turn away but caught sight of Damien striding in her direction. Sander reacted immediately. He could save her one headache at least.

With fists clenched and jaw firmed, he went after his brother. Damien could not evade him forever. Sander snatched his greatcoat from the same efficient butler and met his brother at the carriage.

The redhaired lady was nowhere in sight. Rain soaked his hat, sluiced past his greatcoat, and down his back in icy rivulets.

"You again?" Damien turned away and climbed in the rig.

Sander followed. "We entered the hell together. Remember? Or has your brain degenerated to the point of ashes?"

"Why are you in London, anyway? Don't I have properties that need tending to?"

"You know very well how prosperous your lands are doing under my management." He settled across from his brother. "What is wrong, Damien?" he asked gently, earnestly. "I remember a time not so many years ago when we had one another's back. Is that all gone now?"

Damien fell against the velvet swab. His eyes closed and he ran a palm over his face. "My wife is dying, Sander, if she hasn't already succumbed. She'll not make it through the birth of this child." He spoke on a resigned sigh that slithered through Sander.

"I'm sorry." He hadn't known, having spent the last few months touring the other properties, minding the books, the tenants and all. "Then what *are* you doing in London? The boys need you."

"Only Noah is home. Lucius is away at school, if you'll recall. I'll head back to Stonemare after handling a small matter before departing."

"Is there anything I can do to help?"

A short smile flashed across his face. "Find another governess. Noah's impatience to leave for Eton had him chasing the last one away. I suppose he thinks as long as there is no governess, he won't be forced to wait the full three years until he turns thirteen. And something must be done."

Damien's second son was an avid learner. A voracious reader who took more after Sander than his own sire.

"Perhaps that beautiful harlot you were attempting to rescue is available. She would be quite pleasing to have about." The harsh cynicism had returned to Damien's tone, and Sander's jaw tightened to nearly breaking.

"Don't call her that," he bit out. Then started to refute the idea. "It's an intriguing notion. Unfortunately, I don't know her name."

"Ah." Damien shot him a grin that resembled the devil he was named for.

"Don't sound so smug. I doubt you even remember your own wife's name, if the rumblings about London are to be presumed." Sander's light tone had the desired outcome.

The tension eased slack in Damien's shoulder and his devil smile returned. "I believe Miss Verda Fairclough's dear papa has hopes of snagging Rathbourne for her. She didn't seem too keen, did she?"

"No. She didn't," he agreed softly, assuming she'd even be interested in such a position. If she was indeed on the hunt for a titled husband, then—no, he was almost certain independence was what she most valued. Miss Fairclough at Stonemare? He liked the idea. He liked the idea very much. With Sander there to supervise, of course. "Miss Verda Fairclough, you say?"

Damien nodded.

"I'll see what I can do."

Chapter Four

TONIGHT, VERDA WORE a brilliant, emerald gown with embroidered leaves in gold sewn at the edges of the sleeves, bodice, and hemline. It was the second of her three newest gowns Papa had insisted on last season. Typically, she steered clear of *ton* events. Yet here she sat in a box that belonged to Viscount Harlowe and his viscountess, who'd yet to appear.

"So, you had to make a scene. Rathbourne had you in his sights, in his *grasp*, and you flouted him outright. In front of everyone." The baron's chin jiggled with the fury of his shaking body. "I could not believe my ears."

"I have news for you, Papa," she said in a low hiss. "I have no intention of selling out myself to save you from your foibles. Even if, by some miracle, I find a way to dig you out of debt, you'll just do it again and again." She plopped back against her seat.

"You'll do as I say, Verda."

She shot to her feet, forgetting the crowds below, across, in front of, and behind their box. "If I marry, it shall be on *my* terms. Not yours. If I wish to marry a pig farmer, I'll marry one. Surely, that couldn't be worse than being installed at one of Rathbourne's many holdings with his spoiled daughter he likely hasn't seen since the moment she was born." With a swish of her skirts, she was outside the box in a hall devoid of people to catch her breath. Her heart pounded with an anger only matched by Rathbourne's referring to her as a "piece."

But the anger was overlaid by a thick layer of anxiety. She edged out of the hall to an alcove, clutching the red curtain to allow the air in as she fought to stay on her feet rather than collapsing in a dead faint. Could she really leave her father to collectors and debtors' prison? The thought terrified her. Not just *terrified* her… suffocated her.

The curtain jerked from her fingers. Her gaze flew up. Right into Rathbourne's sneering leer, blocking her exit, the oxygen. Dear heavens, was she to swoon right there?

Verda brought her palms to his chest and shoved, but he proved immovable. She was trapped. She cowered into a corner, black teasing her vision.

Trapped. The trunk blocked the door from the inside. Why couldn't she move it? She was the one who'd shoved it into place. It was too heavy. "Mama!"

But Mama didn't answer and her hands were really cold. The housekeeper wasn't due back until tomorrow.

Tears streamed down her face and she banged on the door and screamed. "Papa, Papa, Papa—"

"Where's your husband now—*Mrs.* Oshea?"

The vileness in his tone rippled over her. She blinked and recoiled, but there was nowhere to go.

A large hand landed on Rathbourne's shoulder and yanked him back. "Right here, Your Grace."

Verda started and her gaze shot to Mr. Oshea's sudden appearance.

The fingers of his large hand dug into the duke's padded shoulder hard enough that the man's grip fell away from her and forced him away from her. "Perhaps my brother was onto something." He let go and dusted his hands together.

The calmness of his tone brought Verda to her senses. She skirted the duke to move behind Mr. Oshea, still trembling, but steadier.

But Mr. Oshea was not finished. "You may be yet dead before the year is out. And, here I thought my brother was jesting. Name your seconds, Rathbourne."

What? "A duel?" Verda found her voice, though she'd have equated it more to the squeal of a frightened mouse. She latched on to Mr. Oshea's arm. "No. I will not be responsible for any injury to your person, sir."

His eyes flashed to hers, his hand flattening on his chest. "Ah, you slay me with your doubt, my dear." His tone had taken on that of Edmund Kean's.

"I fear the wrong person is taking the stage," she muttered.

Rathbourne let out a huff of strained laughter. "Married, Miss Fairclough? You? I think not. Well played, Mr. Oshea. She is not worth a bullet in the gullet."

SANDER GLANCED AT the lady and winced. One did not have to employ clairvoyance to read Miss Fairclough's mind. The blood-red sunset of her hair vibrated the waves of her ire. The sight spellbound him momentarily.

Her sharp hiss snapped his attention back to the duke.

Rathbourne's gaze skimmed and stopped at her low-cut bodice. "Your father is in financial trouble, is he not?"

The gall of the man left Sander speechless. He glanced at Miss Fairclough.

Her cheeks burned. "My father may be a reckless fool," she bit out. "But he is more honorable than a scoundrel like you."

"I am not a man to be trifled with, Miss Fairclough. I require a mother for my daughter and you have an exemplary reputation. All that I require in a wife." His ducal disdain moved over Sander and he sniffed. "Oshea is a second son with no viable prospects of his own. He cannot save your father from his creditors. I can." He straightened away from the wall. "I'll await your answer until nine P.M. tomorrow. Now"—he smoothed his hands over his coat then straightened his neckcloth—"I shall take my leave."

Rathbourne backed away before turning and striding away.

Sander had no notion of what to say in the awkward silence that grew, yet he waited.

Her shoulders slumped. "He's right," she said through a stiffened jaw. "My father has gambled himself into dung territory. He'll never stop and I-I won't have you or anyone rescuing him."

Sander turned and stared after Rathbourne as he disappeared down the wide staircase before turning back to Miss Fairclough, whose gaze remained on the now-empty corridor.

"Well, I suppose I would let Rathbourne take it on if I'm forced into such a horrid fate as to marry *him*," she revised on a huff of pure disgust.

Sander considered her for a long minute. Maybe two. "I have an offer for you."

CHAPTER FIVE

Verda cast a wary glance at Mr. Oshea. "I am not for sale, sir. I have my pride."

Red crawled up the man's neck into his face. "You misunderstand me, madam. You could marry me—"

"Ridiculous," she bit out.

An irritating smile curved his full lips. "Or, perhaps you would consider a governess position. My brother requires such for his younger son. Though I must warn you, he's already chased off at least one."

Startled, she blurted out, "Governess." Then more slowly, "Your brother…"

"You appear educated. More importantly, perhaps, such a position will remove you from London."

That didn't sound so awful—except for the "his brother" part. And that she'd never been a governess before. And that she knew absolutely nothing of children.

"I take it you are not enamored of the duke's attention. Is your father pressuring you to marry the blackguard?"

"No. Yes. Er, how far out of London?"

"Northumberland."

The oxygen expelled from her body in a gush. One couldn't get much farther than northeastern England. "I suppose I'm to leave my father to his fate, no matter how dire?" As tempting as the prospect was, she wasn't certain she had the stomach to leave Papa at the mercy of people she didn't know.

"I would never expect you to, Miss Fairclough."

"Then what am I to do? The situation is hopeless from all sides and will likely never change." Not until he'd departed this Earth. A thought that made her ill. He *was* her father.

A fleeting grin crossed Mr. Oshea's features. "I'm surprised at you, Miss Fairclough. You don't strike me as a woman to see any situation as hopeless."

She suppressed a groan then straightened her spine. *Right.*

"Besides, the confines and strictures at Stonemare are considerably less stringent."

"That does sound appealing," she admitted slowly, her eyes on the toes of her slippers.

"Come, it grows late and I suspect your father is wondering where you've disappeared."

Verda's head snapped up. Good heavens. It had completely slipped her mind that she was standing unchaperoned with a gentleman in a vacant hall at the Theatre Royal with the smell of tallow candles inundating her. Wait—she tilted her head, considering him, this unlikely… man. "How did you know where to find me?"

He offered her another smile and it seemed quite genuine. "Ah. I have Mrs. Dove-Lyon to thank for that. She informed me that you are not the typical young woman to come to her for assistance in looking for a husband. She also said that while you abhor society events, you adore theater."

In all fairness, she'd never approached the woman and wondered how Mrs. Dove-Lyon would know such a thing about her. Yes. It had been Papa's grandiose idea in the first place. Rathbourne had found her as well, and Mr. Oshea's news that Mrs. Dove-Lyon would share such details about her explained everything. Verda cleared her throat. "I see." It also renewed her anger. Papa had nearly compromised her in the worst possible way.

"Return to your father, Miss Fairclough. I'll call for you at your home in the morning and discuss my plan with you at that time." He gave her hand a gentle squeeze. "Things will work out. You shall see." He escorted her to the entrance to the viscount's box then bowed. "Until tomorrow, then. Good night."

Verda entered the box and all eyes turned on her. She murmured her apologies and took the seat next to her father, ignoring his pointed look.

The situation didn't feel quite as hopeless as it had twenty minutes ago.

CHAPTER SIX

A T THE UNGODLY hour of ten o'clock the next morning, Sander was shown into Baron Krupt's shabby parlor by an aging butler. There were few paintings on the walls and even a place or two where it looked as if larger works had been replaced by smaller, less majestic pieces. He veered closer to read the artist's signature. Verda Fairclough. The depiction of a pastoral scene of a chapel, a small graveyard, and sheep. There were dark, low-hanging clouds, but the sun was attempting to win out.

It struck Sander as somewhat metaphorical, considering her statement regarding a hopeless situation. He took in the sorry state of the threadbare curtains and carpet. Dust particles danced in a beam of sunlight from windowpanes that could have used a good scrub.

Miss Fairclough hurried in carrying a tray laden with tea and scones.

Despite the grayish wool frock she wore, a light sheen of perspiration gave her face a dewy, youthful look. And that brilliant shade of her hair mollified any drab gown she could possibly don.

She went to move past him, but he intercepted her, taking the tray. "Where is your housekeeper? You look as if you've been laboring in the kitchens yourself." He set it on a low table, straightened, and glanced at her.

Her back was to him, showcasing interspersed golden highlights he hadn't noticed in their two previous encounters. Hair that hung scandalously to her waist was tied at her nape with a painted ribbon in a delicate pink. That the colors clashed so violently endured her more to him. She turned then and the blush in her cheeks embarrassed him. "I'm sorry—"

"Please." She waved out a hand. "Certainly, you can see how drastic our circumstances have become. If I don't marry Rathbourne, I fear they'll grow worse."

"I'm here to assure you they will not. As I mentioned, my nephew needs a governess. He is anxious to attend school but is not yet of an age. He is above average intelligence." He flashed a grin. "He takes after me."

"I expect he has your charm as well?" she said dryly.

He cleared his throat. "Er, yes. That is a given. Now, about this governess position?"

The small smile disappeared. "As I mentioned before—"

"Yes, yes. I know you've no experience with teaching or children. I still find that you accepting my offer will benefit all concerned," he said, rebutting her with an outfacing palm. "I shall speak to your father."

Her smile did not return and he could guess why. His brother was a whoremonger and her worry was a legitimate one. What should have been gratitude was outright suspicion. "And the earl? Where will he be?"

That was one question Sander did not relish addressing, but he forced himself to answer truthfully. "His wife is in childbed. Her third. As I understand it, he will be returning to Stonemare soon."

She rose stiffly to her feet and spoke briskly. "Then I must respectfully decline, sir. I don't care for the notion of having to lock myself in my chamber in an effort to remain safe from some overindulged peer."

"My brother does not assault unwilling women, I can assure you." There will be no need to lock yourself away in order to save your virtue."

She paced to the grimy windows then back. "Just how sure

are you, sir?"

Sander's lips tightened because she raised a point he did not like to think possible of Damien.

"Lord Pender is a libertine. Tell me, Mr. Oshea. His reputation is well earned throughout the *ton*."

"I shall be accompanying you to Northumberland, Miss Fairclough. You shall be quite safe from my brother." The thought of returning to Stonemare without her couldn't be borne. "Now, let us talk wages."

$$\maltese \quad \text{\small\rule{3cm}{0.4pt}}\!\!\bowtie\!\!\text{\small\rule{3cm}{0.4pt}} \quad \maltese$$

CHAPTER SEVEN

Northumberland—Two Weeks Later

VERDA DRAGGED HER gaze from the window and the horrendous weather bombarding the carriage—that had turned a week's journey into eleven days—to her maid, Lizzie. The poor girl had been released from the Krupt household three years ago due to lack of funds. Then reinstated once Papa had had it in his head for Verda to set her cap for Rathbourne. She hadn't been about to travel to Northumberland alone with Mr. Oshea. Not if she wished to remain unmarried, of which she definitely so wished. In desperation and for propriety's sake, Verda had negotiated for Lizzie to accompany her.

Lizzie clutched the leather strap, wincing at each rut the carriage hit. It would be a miracle if a wheel, or worse, an axel, didn't snap in half and leave them stranded or perished in God-knew-where.

"I expect you're regretting your decision in this little jaunt." Verda clung to another strap as another bump in the road jarred her entire body.

"N-No, m-miss." The poor woman's teeth were chattering. "Mr. Oshea was quite g-generous."

He was that. Of course, now her maid was in Mr. Oshea's employ. Verda thought of the ultimatum Mr. Oshea had issued two weeks ago that she'd stood wholeheartedly behind. Her father now had a live-in manservant to oversee Papa's activities.

His debts settled and a decree of no more excess gambling. Or drinking. Or any of the other vices he might harbor, of which she was likely, and gladly, unaware. She wasn't certain how Mr. Oshea had managed Papa, but she decided his docile behavior would suffice and was grateful for the guilt it had alleviated.

She glanced out at the dark clouds as they barreled toward the cold North Sea—destination Alnmouth—to a residence dubbed Stonemare. Such a name brought to mind a drafty castle straight out of the late Middle Ages. Stone walls, stone floors, no privies, rushes and straw tossed about to warm the floors and absorb disgusting malodors.

Moments later, a large, imposing structure loomed out of the murky sky that would have done *The Castle of Otranto* every sort of justice, though Verda had never cracked the book herself. Her imagination had taken flight from the spell of the horrid novel craze many of her acquaintances from school had fallen under after devouring Mrs. Radcliffe's words. Verda suspected having lived through the terror of being stranded with her dead mother at eight years old had cured her of any desire to relive that horror, fictitious or no, mattered not.

A knock sounded from above and the trapdoor opened. "Never fear, ladies," Mr. Oshea shouted over a howling wind that had Verda grasping for the neck of her cloak to fend off the icy air. "We're within a stone's throw now." Then he laughed—at his awful pun, she supposed—and slapped the trapdoor shut. There was an ominous feel to the silence that followed.

"Will we be safe, ye think, miss?"

Verda's gaze went to Lizzie's face. It was a mere shadow.

She shored up her nerves, raising her chin and steeling her spine. "Of course, we will, Lizzie. Mr. Oshea would never put us in danger." She spoke in her haughtiest tone that revealed only the slightest tremor. "I am here for his nephew and you are here for me. Mr. Oshea promised us so, remember?"

Lizzie's teeth chattered again. Or perhaps they'd never quit.

"Furthermore, you shall reside in an adjoining room to

mine." *Hopefully.* Verda grabbed Lizzie's free hand. "I know it's an odd situation, dear, but we shall persevere together."

"Yes, miss. Thank ye, miss," she whispered.

The coach turned up a large, sweeping drive to an imposing portico of an ancient castle. All that was missing was gargoyles on either side of the entrance. A tall, cadaverous-looking man with longish, stringy, gray hair appeared and despite the hovering clouds, he acted in no hurry. In fact, the slight limp she detected was almost indiscernible. As if he sensed her watching, his gaze flicked to and held hers. She stifled a gasp at the soulless eyes and spectral hollows in his cheeks.

The door slammed back, startling her. "Oh," she breathed. "Mr. Oshea."

He glanced behind him then turned back, smiling. "No, you're not seeing a ghoul. That's Baldric, our stablemaster. He's been at Stonemare for as long as I can recall." He assisted her and Lizzie from the coach. "Hurry now," he said. "It looks to be a magnificent storm brewing."

Though her heart pounded hard enough to rival the oncoming gale, Verda wasted no time. The wind ripped at her skirts, nearly whisking her away. She grabbed Lizzie's hand and they dashed through an open door just as the heavens unleashed buckets of tears. She glanced over her shoulder to see poor Mr. Oshea being doused by the onslaught. Still, the man did not rush forward for cover. He assisted the footmen in handling the baggage and carrying two of the smaller cases.

"Hello." The voice was small. A child's.

Verda spun around. A young boy greeted her. His arms cradled a doll swaddled in blankets. The sight took her aback. "Oh, hello. Master Oshea, I presume?"

"Noah," he confirmed.

She'd never been around children much, and to see a boy holding a doll seemed quite unusual. She moved forward. "May I see your toy?"

His eyes narrowed on her and he stepped back. "No, thank

you. He is not a toy. He's my Julius."

Not a toy?

A squeak emitted from it. "He's hungry," he said. He hugged the tiny being to his thin chest.

"Blast it, Master Noah! Bring that child back right this minute."

Verda's gaze shot to the landing at the top of a grandiose staircase framed by elaborately carved balustrades, from which a large-bosomed woman glared down at them, her beefy hands fisted at her hips.

Without another word or glance back, the boy, Noah, went up the stairs and handed off the child.

"Was that really a baby, ma'am?" Lizzie's voice filtered in, but Verda didn't take her eyes from the landing above, though neither Noah nor the woman were still in sight.

"I don't see how it couldn't be." Verda blinked then slowly circled, taking in their surroundings.

The walls, not of stone, lived up to every dark thought she imagined existed in Mrs. Radcliffe's novels. There was indeed a draft that blasted from the open doors. The cold air did not dispel the taint of mustiness or the earthy scent of stone and old wood. It reminded her a bit of home, actually, and teased her with a bit of ironic humor. Old tapestries hung throughout, depicting hunting scenes, florals and landscapes with water and bridges, and lastly, a joust straight out of the medieval era. Even without touching them, Verda could see the quality was phenomenal.

If the floors were stone, she couldn't tell from the Persian rug she stood upon, though it was worn in places. Flames flickered in sconces along the wall but didn't blow out.

The entryway instantly grew chaotic as Mr. Oshea entered and stomped mud from his boots. A harried housekeeper appeared, righting her white mobcap. "Ye must be the new governess for Master Noah. 'E'll be excited to meet ye."

Verda gave a small smile but didn't bother informing her that she'd met the young master already and he hadn't appeared in the least eager for his upcoming lessons. Perhaps she was wrong, but as she'd warned Mr. Oshea, she knew nothing of children.

"Come along. I'll show ye to yer rooms. Don' know where Mr. Winfield is at present. We run a skeleton crew 'ere, miss."

"Mr. Winfield?"

"The butler, miss. Useless bastard," she muttered under her breath, though not low enough to keep Verda from making out every word.

She met Lizzie's startled eyes. Verda gave a small shake of her head. "Of course. I'd like my maid to reside nearby, if it's no trouble," Verda told her.

The older woman stopped and peered over her shoulder at them. "I see. Well, changes things a bit." Then she grinned an almost toothless smile. "O'course, o'course. No problem a'tall." She turned and continued up the stairs.

Relief spilled through Verda as she and Lizzie continued following the robust woman on up.

"I'll have your bags sent up in nothing flat," Mr. Oshea called out from below.

At the sound of his cheerful countenance, Verda nearly tripped, but Lizzie gripped her arm, saving her from a mortifying fate.

"I'm Mrs. Knagg," the woman said, apparently oblivious to any mishap. "I reckon Master Noah will be anxious to get back t'his studies. Never seen a child so enthralled with learnin', that be the truth."

Mrs. Knagg took them up past the first floor to the family rooms on the second floor and down a long hall, through a gallery, to another wing. East, possibly.

She opened a door to a bedchamber fit for a… a queen, if it had been cleaned and readied. "Here ye are, miss. I'll send one o'the footmen to light the fire for ye." She smiled, exposing a missing tooth.

"But, this is… is much too… grand…"

"'Tis the only one with a sittin' room and chamber for yer

maid. Ye'll settle in nicely. We ain't so particular in these parts, miss. 'Spect his lordship will want t'visit with ye on the morrow. Dinner's at seven in the small dinin' room."

"Er, Mrs. Knagg. Will there be someone to guide me to the small dining room? And what of Lizzie's dinner?"

Mrs. Knagg glanced over her shoulder with another grin. "O'course, miss. One o'the maids'll call fer ye." Her eyes went over Lizzie. "Servants' stairs are down the hall. They lead straight to the kitchens. Ye can't miss 'em."

"Thank you, Mrs. Knagg."

After the housekeeper's departure, Verda went to the hearth. There was a flint and striking stone on the mantle. She lowered to her knees and, aiming the flint toward the kindling, she struck. The sparks flew onto the kindling on the first strike. She leaned in and blew. Seconds later, a small flame caught hold.

"I'm always amazed at your abilities, miss," Lizzie said, shaking her head.

Verda grinned. She'd never explained her reasoning for learning such a skill, and she didn't now, either. She toured her "suite" and was pleased to find a small sitting room and even a room for Lizzie. The wardrobe was large with more pegs than Verda required.

There was a knock. More like a pounding.

"Enter," she said.

"Miss Fairclough." Mr. Oshea came in carrying hers and Lizzie's smaller bags, followed by a footman hoisting Verda's trunk on his shoulders. "I understand Mrs. Knagg offered you different accommodations than those originally prepared for you."

"My maid—"

He set down their bags then waved out his hand. "No need to explain. My apologies on not considering beforehand."

The footman appeared in the door and she quickly stepped back. "Goodness."

He unloaded her trunk then strode to the hearth. "The fire's lit," he said, tilting his head and looking confused.

"Thank you, Fletcher." Mr. Oshea rubbed his hands together as if he hadn't heard the man. Then he frowned. "It shouldn't take long to warm things up. I must admit, this wing of the castle is not typically occupied."

"Which makes it perfect to have my maid nearby." Her heart hammered against her ribs. They did not appear to be starting off on a good footing. "Besides," she rationalized… a little heatedly. "I have need of her assistance and you did promise." She didn't care to explain in front of Lizzie or the footman that with Lizzie's presence, there was an added protection in the event Lord Pender stumbled in—inadvertently, of course.

Mr. Oshea inclined his head and let her explanation stand.

Verda ignored him and glanced about then realized she stood amidst her bedchamber with an unmarried man. It was suddenly, definitely warm now. "Perhaps we should adjourn to the sitting room."

A grin fleeted his features that was almost wolfish. Perhaps it was the gloom invading the room from the windows. "I shall take my leave." He moved to the door. "I'll arrange for you to meet with Noah tomorrow morning. He'll be very excited."

"Actually, I've already made the acquaintance of Master Noah. I must say, he did not appear thrilled. And while we are about the subject of meeting the household, Mrs. Knagg has informed me that Lord Pender also wishes to meet with me in the morning."

"Mrs. Knagg is a busybody. We shall speak at dinner, which is at seven."

The door latched softly, drawing a smirk from her. After a second, it shifted into a full-blown smile, then she shook her head and followed Lizzie to inspect the rest of the lovely, unprepared suite.

THE CASTLE'S DINING chamber held the oldest piece of furniture in the keep: a scarred, wooden table with carved legs and clawed feet. Grand portraits that could stand a thorough cleaning glared down at him. There was a miniscule number of servants despite the estate's holdings. In the event they needed additional staff, Mrs. Knagg hired extras from Alnmouth, which was rarely the case. The situation suited Sander fine, though the reasons behind that were irritating at best—the villagers believed Stonemare haunted. Lady Pender's recent demise only added to its eerie notoriety.

Sander took his place at the far end of the table opposite Damien's chair. His brother hadn't yet appeared, but then neither had Miss Fairclough. With a sigh, he slipped the fob from his waistcoat and opened it. Seven-oh-two. Shutting it with a snap, he dropped it back in its allotted pocket then picked up his wine. He set it to his lips as the doors swung wide and Fletcher appeared. The footman stepped aside, allowing Miss Fairclough to enter.

The magnificent countenance of her bearing stole the breath from Sander's chest with a formidable assault to his sternum. Without a single touch of the wine, his glass landed hard on the table, though he managed to rise slowly, calmly to his feet. He inclined his head. "Miss Fairclough."

"Mr. Oshea."

"You look"—*ravishing, delectable, captivating*—"very nice."

"Thank you." She glanced at the table. "Where is Lord Pender?"

"I haven't seen him as of yet." He shrugged. "That is not entirely out of the ordinary for him." Likely, he was passed out in his chamber from too much spirits, but Sander didn't say so aloud. He strolled to the new governess and held out his arm. "Fletcher, move Miss Fairclough's setting to my right, please. There's no need for us to shout at one another halfway across the room."

She laid her hand on his and he led her to the table. "I'm not sure this is at all proper," she said, frowning.

"Here in Northumberland, we are on the edges of society. Practically Scotland. And everyone knows the Scots are savages."

"I sincerely hope you are joking," she said as primly as a governess should sound.

"I believe you shall make an excellent governess," he teased.

She wrinkled her nose. "I suppose that's my tendency to instruct those around me to do my bidding."

"Sounds ominous." *And interesting.*

"The bane of Papa's existence, I assure you."

The meal was the most memorable in Sander's memory. He could barely keep his eyes from the brilliance of that hair. Her gown was not that of a proper governess, either, he was thrilled to note. The green was emerald, but not silk. That would have been too much to ask.

"Will you tell me something of my charge?" she asked.

"Noah? He's well read. A little gentleman."

"Why does he carry an infant about? I was concerned he might drop it, er…him? Her?"

"A boy. Noah's attached and has been very attentive. He refuses to let anyone other than the wet nurse care for him."

"His mother perished, after all, then." The soft sympathy of her voice caressed his skin as if it were her fingers.

"Yes. I wasn't here at the time. Before London, I was making my annual rounds of the other Pender properties."

"I don't know much about—"

Sander looked her full in her blushing face. He smiled, feeling a bit ornery. "Children? So you've said. Let me tell you something, Miss Fairclough. There is no need to keep reminding me. I am aware of whom I hire, and I'm happy with my selection. So, you will cease acting as if I will dismiss you on the spot." When, in fact, he wanted nothing more than to show her exactly how he wanted her.

She dropped her gaze to her plate. "Thank you for the assurances, Mr. Oshea. I hope you don't regret your choice. I'm sure I will commit many faux pas in the days to come."

"And I'll forgive each and every one," he said with a quick grin.

VERDA STORMED INTO her chamber, furious with herself for letting Lizzie talk her into wearing the emerald muslin. How the devil was she supposed to know what a governess wore to dinner? Her own had been dismissed when she had been but a child herself. Her vague memories yielded little helpful information. Gads, she wanted to scream.

Lizzie entered on her heels. "Oh, dear. What is it, miss? You're upset."

"I told you this ridiculous gown was inappropriate." She dropped her shawl. "Help me out of it. Then I want you to stuff it in the back of the wardrobe. Better yet, toss it in the grate. We can use it as fuel." She could barely keep her feet still long enough for Lizzie to unfasten the myriad buttons down the back. She stepped out of the infernal gown and stomped to the bed, pulling back the coverlets—and let out an abrupt screech.

Lizzie rushed over. "What is it—oh."

Verda couldn't speak. Not with one hand covering her mouth, and the other pointing to the center of the soft-looking sheets.

"Ah, miss, 'tis only a lizard and its offspring."

She gasped. "But... they're blue."

"They won't hurt ye, miss." Lizzie went to the bed and, to Verda's shock, scooped it and its three "offspring" in her hand.

"Will you put them outside?" she asked, surprised that she still stood upright and hadn't yet fainted.

"Oh, no, miss. It's much too cold." Lizzie looked at the little critters, her nose wrinkled. "I suspect they're pets. Otherwise, they'd have scattered like the wind."

The thought nearly buckled Verda's knees. "I can't sleep in that bed." She gripped the table to steady herself. "You'll sleep in here. I'll take your bed."

"But—"

"No *buts*. I absolutely insist. Now dispense with... with..." She waved out her hand.

"Of course, miss."

CHAPTER EIGHT

W INFIELD, RATHER *MR.* Winfield—she had to remember she was part of the household as a staff member, not the lady of the house—the butler as old as the hills, led Verda to the earl's study at precisely ten o'clock the next morning as instructed by the note sitting on the escritoire in her chamber. Exhaustion pelted her. Lizzie's bed was horribly lumpy. And while Verda had slept little, it was more than she would have had she been forced to sleep in her own bed, imagining left-behind reptiles. Shuddering, she waited as Mr. Winfield tapped on the study door then entered on a muffled "Come in."

She followed inside to yet another darkened room. There was a logical explanation for the gloom: the windows were draped in black in respect for the late Lady Pender.

Floor-to-ceiling bookcases lined two walls and a blazing fire in the grate did little to stave off the chill that went bone deep. Stacks of papers covered the desk along with inkwells and quills. A globe sat on one corner. A lantern on the other.

The earl's head was bent where she could see only the top of his dark hair.

He looked up. "Good morning."

An unfamiliar leap in Verda's chest stuttered to an odd wobbling. "Oh, Mr. Oshea." *Too breathless.* She glanced quickly about, but the genuine Lord Pender was nowhere to be seen. On hesitant steps, she moved forward.

He grimaced. "It appears my brother has left the premises."

"I see. And that affects me…how, exactly? I mean, do you require his signature or something?"

"Not at all, Miss Fairclough. His departure changes nothing. I thought you might be concerned. I didn't learn he'd left until Winfield mentioned it this morning."

She waved a hand in the direction of the windows. "How odd with the house in mourning."

He cleared his throat. "Er, yes. As the gossipmongers report, my brother rarely acts as decorum dictates."

White-hot embarrassment rushed through her veins. She swallowed a groan. "I-I'm sorry. I often speak before I think. Much too often," she muttered under her breath.

"Please. As I told you last night, I'd been in Cornwall. So, things are a little dubious around here," he responded. "I believe it was not unpredicted."

"I expect that's why Master Noah has taken on the position of nursemaid."

Mr. Oshea's gaze flickered his surprise. "Nursemaid?"

"I mentioned meeting him. In the vestibule upon our arrival yesterday," she reminded him.

"Yes. Yes," he said, impatience seeming to ripple over him. "Again, that is neither here nor there. But… he had the infant—"

The door opened and Verda turned.

Mr. Oshea stopped mid-sentence. "Excellent, Noah. I appreciate your promptness." He rose from behind the desk and, rounding it, went to the seating area before the hearth. "Shall we sit?"

Verda took a seat on the settee, cutting a side glance at her new charge, who incidentally, entered empty handed—meaning… no infant.

Mr. Oshea took the wingback chair, forcing Noah beside her. He did his best to jam himself as close to the arm as he could get without sitting on it. He slid her a wary look, likely thinking of the little gift he'd planted in her bed the night before.

She met that glance and held it. "Do you have pets, Master

Noah?"

"Er, no."

Sympathy touched Mr. Oshea's forehead. He leaned forward and set a hand on Master Noah's knee. "I'm saddened to hear that, Noah. You've had your lizards for neigh on five years now, isn't it?"

Noah's—*Master Noah*, she silently reminded herself. His ears flamed red and he shifted uncomfortably, *as well he should*, and quickly turned to Mr. Oshea. "Am I in trouble, Uncle Sander?"

A fleeting wince flashed Mr. Oshea's features before he affected as haughty a tone as any lord she'd ever heard. "Certainly not."

"Where is Papa?"

"He departed this morning. He mentioned you were upset about not attending school with Lucius." Mr. Oshea narrowed his eyes on the boy. "Are you?"

"Not any longer." Master Noah's gaze raked over her and he crossed his arms before turning back to his uncle.

Verda's stomach dipped. She was going to have to leave. Her new life was over before it had begun. With her and Lizzie bound for London on the next mail coach. At least she wouldn't find a family of lizards in her bed. *No, the workhouse would house big, fat rats.*

"Why not?" Mr. Oshea asked calmly.

"I have to take care of the baby. Papa told me so."

Mr. Oshea rubbed his forehead. "Noah," he said gently, "there is a wet nurse. You are a child. You can hardly care for an infant."

Oh, dear. Verda held her breath watching as the young master's hands squeezed into fists until his knuckles whitened. She made a silent vow to have Lizzie return his "pets" right away.

Noah shot to his feet. "I *can* take care of him. Papa gave him to *me*."

"All right, all right. Calm down. I'm not here to take your new brother away from you, son."

Master Noah's lips tightened and he remained rigid as a board. Strangely enough, Mr. Oshea's expression mirrored his nephew's.

After a long moment, the tension in the room lowered and he narrowed his eyes on his uncle. "Where *is* Papa?"

"I've no idea. I'm as frustrated as you, to be sure. Now, please sit down and remember your manners. There is a young woman present."

Master Noah slowly resumed his place on the settee.

"Miss Fairclough has graciously consented to being your governess until such time you leave for Eton."

The boy's lips compressed and he narrowed his eyes on Verda. "I'm not learning embroidery."

"Thank goodness for that. As it happens, I cannot stitch a straight line to save my life," she said, keeping her voice strictly matter-of-fact.

The surprise on Noah's face had her biting the inside of her cheek to keep from smiling.

"I would love to hear more about these"—she speared Mr. Oshea a questioning glance—"lizards, you say?"

"Noah is quite the caretaker," he returned.

"Even for a family of lizards…" she muttered under her breath.

"What's that? I didn't hear you," Mr. Oshea said.

She ignored that. "So… no embroidery, then, we are agreed. Is there a particular subject you prefer to another?" she asked young Noah.

"Well, I have been reading *The Sceptical Chymist*." He spoke the words as a challenge. "I'm going to set up a laboratory."

"Interesting," she murmured. "I, too, have read some on the subject."

Master Noah's eyes widened in a look of sheer disbelief.

"It's true. Elizabeth Fulhame did chemistry experiments in the late 1700s on dyeing methods."

His mouth fell open. "A woman?"

She grinned at him. "Women have brains too, you know. Or haven't your own studies mentioned that nugget of information?"

Noah's mouth snapped shut. Only for a moment. "What does *dying* have to do with chemistry?" he demanded.

"She studied a method of infusing cloth with metals. Gold, silver…" She lifted a shoulder. "Metals of that sort."

"To put on a dead body?" His incredulity had her swallowing a laugh. He was quite bright. She wondered briefly if that was normal for most children.

Verda stole a look at Mr. Oshea, who reclined back in his chair with his hands flattened on muscular thighs, momentarily distracting her. Her eyes moved up to see his lips tipped on one end. Cheeks flaming, and with an internal shake of her head, she went on. "No. Not dying as in expiring from life. Dyeing as in working with fabrics. Changing their colors and such."

"Oh, that's nothing," he said with a smugness that sent her own blood rising in a heated temperature.

"You think so?" She curled her fingers and pretended to study her nails, being careful to remain nonchalant. "Mrs. Fulhame published a book on her findings in 1794."

"I bet you're lying—"

"Noah!" Mr. Oshea barked.

"Apologies, ma'am. But a woman writing a book on chemistry. That doesn't seem likely to me. What is it called?"

"I can't remember the exact title. It's very long, cumbersome, even, but it has something to do with new art and painting wherein hypotheses are proved erroneous or some such incoherence. Truly, it is a ridiculously long title."

A thoughtful glint gleamed in his eye. "If she did write a book on chemistry, then it's probably in our library."

"We shall look and if we cannot locate it, I shall pen a note to my father and have him send along my copy."

"Thank you," he said graciously.

"Now, what of our schedule, Master Noah? Is there a particular time that will work for you so that I may earn my wages?"

The wary look reappeared. "I suppose I could work while my Julius takes his morning and afternoon naps. I may have to bring him to my lessons. He doesn't like it if I'm too far away when he wakes."

"Brilliant. We shall begin this afternoon. What time does he nap?" she asked.

"It varies."

She was on to him now. "Then I shall meet you in the school-room, say two of the clock?"

Noah glanced at Mr. Oshea, who gave a slight incline of his head. "That will be acceptable," Noah said. He stood and turned to his uncle. "May I be excused, sir? I must check on my Julius."

"Of course. Thank you for your time, Noah."

Noah gave a proper bow in Verda's direction. "Thank you, ma'am. I should be very interested in learning what Mrs. Fulhame has to say regarding dyeing. Even though it would be more exciting if she wrote about expiring."

"I expect it would," Verda agreed. "Perhaps you can show me these, um, lizards of yours."

Red crawled up his neck and tipped his ears, his eyes flickered away. "They, um, ran away."

"Oh? That seems a shame. I shall ask my maid if she's happened upon them. Until this afternoon, then."

Master Noah dashed out of the room as if fire licked at his heels.

"What an unusual young man," she said to Mr. Oshea. "He seems quite dedicated to his new brother."

Mr. Oshea's gaze was on the closed door. "Yes. I suspect it's due to his mother's recent passing." He turned back to Verda. "What was all that business regarding lizards? I was not aware that women had an interest in reptiles of any sort."

"Perhaps I'm unlike any of the women you've ever met."

His eyes darkened with an intensity that had her tempted to run out of the room in the same fashion as young Noah. She rose from the settee. "Well, if you'll excuse me as well, I should like to take in some air."

He frowned somewhat fiercely. "Do not stray far. The weather can turn treacherous in an instant. Not to mention the cliffs."

Every independent hackle Verda possessed prickled along her skin. "It seems the men as well as the children in this family have not reconciled their thinking toward the idea that women indeed harbor brains of their own." Glimpsing the bemused glint in his eyes seemed the perfect time for a timely exit.

She turned on her heel and escaped. She didn't want to *like* him.

THE CLICK OF the door echoed. Sander stood, went to the windows, and pushed aside the black covering representing the most recent death—after all, his parents had also perished at this very property. Father right there on the moors where Verda was determined to walk.

Breath held, he waited for her to appear as this side of the house didn't face the front, but the worn path did. He waited… and waited until his hand clenched into a fist from the strain and he was forced to relax and flex his fingers.

He started to turn away, determined to go after her when he caught sight of her hair. Its flaming beacon allowed him to breathe. Miss Verda Fairclough was a most unusual woman and he was as taken with her now as he had been in London. She was as bold and forthright as that fiery hair of hers. But she was as out of his reach as the stars hidden behind the leaden clouds he was looking at. Secrets were horrible determents.

Frustrated with this line of thought, Sander turned his mind to Noah and another disturbing dilemma. The boy's attachment to his new brother struck a chord deep in Sander. How close he and Damien had been as children. The memories were painful and Sander refused to dwell on them, but something had changed. Not that Damien had ever been predictable. There was the time not long before Father had died that Damien had appeared in the door of the schoolroom, his nose bloodied and broken. Sander had stormed down four flights of stairs. Sander had always been bigger and stronger than Damien. And their father had hated Damien—

Something had happened since Sander's last visit to Stonemare, even before the countess's death. His brother appeared more enigmatic than usual. His nephew defensive and outright combative. It was a blessing, he supposed, that Lucius was away at school. One less worry on Sander's mounting pile.

It was past time he met this newest addition to the Oshea clan. The black covering fell from his grip and he left the study for the third floor where the nursery and the schoolroom were located.

Sander knocked on Noah's chamber door, but there was no answer. He peered in the schoolroom. No fire blazed in the hearth and it was frigid. He made a note to avail the library for Noah's lessons with Miss Fairclough. It didn't hurt that he could visit at will with less speculation for his motives. *Of which there were none.*

After glancing in another couple of chambers, Sander found Noah sitting with the wet nurse enthralled, and not at all embarrassed at the baby's suckling of the woman's large breast. Sander, however, could have fallen through the floor. He did his utmost to keep his eyes on the woman's face.

"Noah, your lessons with Miss Fairclough will be held in the library."

"Why?" he asked without looking away from the infant.

An impatient snort erupted from him. "So I can keep an eye on you since you insist on keeping a newborn with you."

Noah shrugged. "All right."

"Mrs.—"

"Lyall, yer lordship."

"Er, my brother is his lordship, Mrs. Lyall. I am Mr. Oshea or 'sir.'" This wasn't the first time he'd had to remind her. "I would like to visit with you as well. The study will do. Noah can escort you after you, er, ah…"

She grinned, clearly tickled with his awkwardness. "I'll be there, sir."

He pulled himself together. One shouldn't feel mortification for a natural part of life.

Mrs. Lyall's chuckle seemed to vibrate against the shut door.

CHAPTER NINE

THE GRAY DAY with its bracing wind enthralled Verda. Though eerie, a state of things she routinely avoided, there was something about the crash of the waves against the rocks below. There was a stark beauty to such barren land. Snow covered parts of the moor while it had melted away and left tiny waterfall rivulets in other places. She could have been the only person in the world.

"Hullo."

Verda swung around, nearly losing her footing on an icy patch, and found herself facing an older man who likely hadn't seen a bath in two years with scraggly, gray-streaked locks and an overgrown beard. He held a long, crooked walking stick.

She took a careful step back. "Um, hello."

"Ain't ne'er seen ye afore. Who are ye?"

"I'm Verda Fairclough. Governess to Master Noah."

He grunted then narrowed rheumy eyes on her. "More liken a mistress to his papa, I'll wager." He shook his head at some long-lost memory trying to break through. "Man ne'er could keep that pikestaff o'is in 'is pantaloons."

Verda straightened to her obnoxious height, towering over him. "I am no man's mistress, sir." Then curiosity got the better of her. "Pikestaff? What do you mean?"

"Babes running about the moors all willy-nilly." He banged his stick on the ground.

His mistresses? More than one? "Um, who might you be, sir?"

He tugged on his beard. "They call me 'Cracked Colbert.'" He gave an elaborate bow that threatened his balance but for his hold on his staff. "Ye can call me 'Cracked.'" He let out a harsh, raspy laugh.

"I'll do no such thing, Mr. Colbert." She dipped a shallow curtsy. "It's nice to make your acquaintance."

"Ain't ne'er been called 'mister' afore, miss. Pleased to make yer 'quaintence." His gaze surveyed the landscape. "Wot ye doing out 'ere alone? 'Tis dangerous."

"It can hardly be dangerous, sir. There's no one here but the two of us."

He chuckled and it sent a chill snaking up her spine. "Quite shur that's wot the old earl thought all those years back."

Her brows beetled. "The old earl? Lord Pender? I met him not three weeks ago in London."

He gave out a hiss of impatience. "The papa. Found frozen t'death not far from where yer standin'."

Verda gasped. "His father? Was found…"

"If'n ye ask me, He was led astray. Poisoned an' left t'die. Townsfolk believe the place is haunted by his spirit."

Well, that explained the lack of adequate number of servants, she supposed. Verda released a long breath that fogged the air and culminated into an unladylike snort. "Haunted? That doesn't sound likely, sir."

"'Tis true, missy. There's trouble a'brewin' at that there castle, mind. Gots t'run now. Makin' me rounds. I'd get on back t'London if'n I was ye. Fast as ye can. Nothin' at Stonemare but bad blood." He ambled away, his voice carrying on the cold wind. "Nothin' but bad blood. But ain't no one been askin' me…"

Verda stood watching, listening to Mr. Colbert's nonsensical words until long after he'd disappeared from sight. The cold air seeped through her coat to her bones. Shivering, she turned back toward the castle and nearly bumped into the spectral—er, *oh, dear,* his name failed her. Then, "Oh, Mr. Baldric, you startled me."

"Jes Baldric, miss. I ain't no 'mister.' Best stay away from ole Colbert." His voice was as gruff as his appearance and gritted over her cold skin like sanded paper. With the dark clouds overhead, all she could make out was his moving mouth. A moving mouth in a face so dark, it faded into the blackening sky. "He ain't stable. Some say he killed the old master."

"W-What?"

But he didn't answer. He was already sauntering away with that hitch she'd noticed before, his stringy, gray hair flying in the sudden gusts.

Verda ran for the castle and stumbled right into Mr. Oshea.

"I wondered if you'd gotten lost," he said, without a trace of his previous charm. His hands warmed her upper arms through her cloak.

She swallowed hard, looking in the direction of the stable-master. But he'd disappeared with the wind.

"I-I can hardly get lost with the tower looming over the land, c-can I?" Her usually firm voice came out breathless and faded in the wake of Baldric.

A plop of icy rain hit her nose.

"Blast it." His hand slid down and gripped hers. "Hurry. There's another storm brewing and there's no shelter for miles but the castle." He yanked her into a run.

She didn't hesitate. She picked up her skirts and ran.

Once inside the foyer, she handed off her cloak and gloves to the aging butler, Mr. Winfield, as no footman seemed about. She shivered.

Mr. Oshea's austere demeanor hadn't abated one iota. "Your lessons with Noah shall be conducted in the library."

She rubbed her hands over her arms, choosing to ignore the unexpected grimness. "Why not the schoolroom?"

"If Noah is determined to have the infant along, the library is a much better option. For one thing, it's warmer. This damnable castle is nothing short of a medieval hovel standing long after its allotted time. It's a wonder it hasn't crumbled into a pile of sand. I don't know why Damien is determined to house Noah and his new son here. They would be infinitely more comfortable in London."

Verda couldn't agree more. Still, there was a stark beauty in the wildness of Northumberland's vast loneliness, if she could discount the mysterious Mr. Colbert's and Baldric's sudden appearances.

Mrs. Knagg greeted them with her gap-toothed smile. "Reckon ye'll be wantin' some tea."

"That would be lovely," Verda told her.

"I'll have chocolate prepared too, for the boy. And scones. He likes Cook's scones." She disappeared toward the back of the house. "Come, I'll show you to the library. There is a fire where you can warm yourself."

Verda pushed Mr. Oshea's odd change of mood from her mind. "That sounds lovely." She entered the library, excitement swirling through her at the notion of earning her own money.

The library was as dark as the rest of the castle, but there was a familiarity with the floor-to-ceiling bookcases that warmed her throughout. The heavily covered windows and blazing fire helped too. She took one of the lanterns and perused the books. The number was astounding. Papa's and her collection had dwindled. Paying one's debts took precedence.

She ran a fingertip along the spines of Homer, Shakespeare, agriculture, poetry, and, ah—she tugged out a book, then smiled. *The Sceptical Chymist.*

"Good afternoon, Miss Fairclough."

Verda glanced over her shoulder and her stomach dipped slightly at the basket he held with two hands. "Hello, Master Noah."

He'd closed the door behind him. "I-I owe you an apology."

"Oh?"

"It was me. I put the lizards in your bed, ma'am. I thought you were here to take away my Julius."

"Take him away?" Shock rippled through Verda. What in

heavens did he think she'd do with an infant? "And you don't believe that any longer?"

"No, ma'am."

She studied him for a long time; suspected it was something more, but it was enough that he'd owned up to his actions, and she'd settle for that. "Then the subject is closed," she said briskly. She held up the book. "I found *The Sceptical Chymist.*" She lowered her arm and met him in the middle of the room. "I see you've brought company. May I have the pleasure of an introduction?"

Noah set the basket down, reached in and lifted an extremely small baby. His eyes were open and his tiny fingers were curled into a fist. One he was attempting to draw to his mouth, but he was stayed by Noah's hold on him. "My Julius, this is Miss Fairclough. She is here to teach us chemistry."

"How nice to meet you, sir. I understand you have a very attentive brother."

Julius emitted a soft coo.

"You can hold him if you like," Noah told her.

Verda quickly straightened. "Thank you, Noah. Another time, perhaps. Shall we get started?"

SANDER LEANED BACK in this chair behind his brother's desk, steepling his fingers and eyeing the broad wet nurse standing before him. He tilted his head. "Is there some reason you feed the infant in front of the child?"

Her raucous belly laugh bounded against the walls.

"I wasn't aware I said something humorous, Mrs. Lyall."

She cleared her throat but couldn't disguise the mirth in her eyes. "It's like this, ye see. The infant is hungry and the child refuses to leave him in me care."

Sander let out a long sigh. He leaned forward and set his

forearms against the hardwood edge of the desk, then met her eyes—pointedly. "Do you believe it appropriate for a child to witness... witness—" Good God, this was mortifying.

"Me tit in the babe's 'ungry mouth?" She gave him a smug smile. "We all started out that a way, Mr. Oshea. Even ye, I reckon."

She had him there.

With an impatient snort, she said, "Lookee, sir, the babe was hungry, an' I was hired to feed 'im. If'n ye don't want the boy there, keep 'im outta the nursery."

"I could let you go without wages," he threatened.

"That ye could. But the babe's a sickly one and I'm one o' the few wet nurses in the region." She shook her massive head, sending her mobcap wiggling precariously. "I doubt 'e'll make it through 'is first year." She narrowed accusing eyes on him. "Ain't no one showed the slightest care for 'im but that boy."

Another excellent point.

"But if'n ye can keep 'im outta o' the nursery," she went on, "'tis yer business, not mine."

"All right," he relented. "Thank you for your time. I'll see what I can do."

Her laugh bellowed once again. "Don't mind me none. Master Noah is an entertainin' fella. Wise beyond 'is years, I reckon."

Sander excused her and sat back in his chair, swiveling it toward the black clouds lowering in the sky. Perhaps Miss Fairclough could offer a suggestion regarding Noah's unusual fascination with the baby.

Hell, Sander couldn't even remember the infant's name. Mrs. Lyall was right—no one outside of Noah had even showed the least amount of interest. He was a horrible uncle.

Sander shoved away from the desk and stalked out of the study to the library, then hesitated at the door. What did he really know of Miss Verda Fairclough?

Almost nothing. He'd hired her—correction—*his* cock had hired her. *That's right*, he admitted. He couldn't quite suppress the image of all that brilliant hair splayed across his pillows. She might not even be qualified to instruct Noah, who could likely instruct *her*. Well, that was unfair. Obviously, she was qualified since she'd taught himself and Noah that women indeed possessed brains. Still, unable to resist, he cracked the door.

Soft murmuring reached him and he let himself in.

The sight took him aback. The lady was seated at a scuffed table. Noah stood at her elbow, their heads together, each holding a piece of graphite. The biggest surprise was the abacus in the middle of the table.

"I don't understand what this has to do with chemistry," Noah said.

"Ah. Well, what if you calculate the measurements incorrectly for a specific formula? Why, you could blow up the entire castle!"

Noah's eyes widened into large, black circles. "I could?"

"Yes. And that would be devastating," she said firmly.

Sander wasn't so sure. At least where Stonemare was concerned. He eased forward to hear more, watching, fascinated, as her fingers moved across the abacus.

"It's quite simple, really. You begin by assigning each column a value. We shall start with something simple." Her fingers stopped. "Do you see that?" She was watching Noah.

His brows were furrowed in fierce concentration.

"When you start, all of the beads in this top row should be in the up position, the ones in the bottom down. See?"

Noah nodded, never taking his eyes from the device.

"Now," she went on, "the beads in the top row represent the number five and each bead in the bottom row represents the number value of one." Miss Fairclough's voice was soft, gentle. Never once did Sander detect condescension. Soon, she had Noah's fingers within her own, showing him how and when to move one bead to its new position, all the while explaining the process of counting.

Within moments, the gleam of enlightenment lit Noah's eyes.

A satisfied grin touched Miss Fairclough's lips that had Sander tempted to send Noah on his way so Sander could devour the woman. She leaned back in her chair, setting her crossed arms on the table in a move that appeared triumphant. "Now, you try it, *using* the abacus." She called out two numbers for him to add.

Noah's fingers weren't as nimble as Miss Fairclough's, but he painstakingly counted out the formula she'd given him to solve.

"Excellent," she breathed. "You have the makings of a very fine mathematician, Master Noah." She put her hands together and softly clapped.

Sander did the same, startling the teacher and her pupil.

"Did you see me, Uncle Sander? I did it."

"I did, indeed."

Noah's exuberance woke the baby and he emitted a tiny cry.

Sander struggled to recall the baby's name, but all he could remember was Noah repeating, "my something," and he was fairly certain "My Something" was not something one called a child.

"Oh. My Julius needs me." Noah's excitement didn't wane as he hurried to the basket near the seating area before the hearth and lifted out the child, who immediately calmed.

Julius. Sander pounded the name in his brain. He watched his elder nephew, intrigued at Noah's handling the infant as efficiently as a well-seasoned nursemaid. Noah sauntered back to the table.

Curiously, panic flashed Miss Fairclough's expression. "That's just fine, Noah. I think we can use a small break." Her small smile didn't fool Sander in the least. That baby terrified her.

Noah grinned at her. "Thank you, Miss Fairclough." He patted the baby's back. "I'd better see to his changing. I'll return soon."

Miss Fairclough rose from the table and picked up the abacus as the door shut behind his nephews. She carried it to a less-filled shelf.

"The infant frightens you?" Sander asked.

He watched her set the abacus on the bookshelf, wondering if she planned to answer him at all.

After a moment, she glanced over her shoulder. "What? No, of course not." She turned back to the abacus and arranged it in an angled fashion. "I just don't know much about children." She made her way back across the library to the seating area and nudged the empty basket aside with the toe of her slipper before sitting down. "I believe this may be the third time I've mentioned this to you," she said wryly.

"So you have."

"Is it me"—Verda's gaze settled on the basket then back up—"or does Master Noah take a more than typical interest in the baby?"

Mr. Oshea's jaw tightened. "You are not mistaken. I find it highly unusual."

"I wonder why," she said softly.

Something Sander had every intention of learning himself.

CHAPTER TEN

One Week Later

"OPEN THE DOOR. *Open the door.*" Verda was screaming and for the life of her, she couldn't stop. "Papa, please." The tears streamed down her face, blinding her. Her candle had run out two days ago, the fire the day before that. "Get it open!" Cold seeped in from the windows of Mama's chamber. Every frock from Mama's closet Verda could reach covered Mama to keep her warm. But Mama hadn't spoken in three days—

"Ma'am. Wake up."

Verda bolted straight up to a fire blazing in the hearth, heavy curtains blocking out the cold, Northumberland winds, a pounding on her chamber door, and the blended cries of an infant and a persistent boy. *Noah.*

She jumped from Lizzie's narrow bed, grabbed her wrapper, and dashed through her original chamber. Lizzie was soundly sleeping in the massive bed. Verda jerked the door open and stopped. "Master Noah? What is it? What's wrong?" An overwhelming sense of dread sent her heart in erratic palpitations.

He fell against her yet managed to hold on to the crying Julius. "He's hungry, ma'am."

Verda cupped his shoulder. Such a tiny frame for the weight he'd taken on for his brother. "Where is Mrs. Lyall, darling?"

"I-I couldn't wake her. I don't know what to do."

Lizzie appeared next to her, wearing only her shift.

Panic infused Verda's blood in sharp, breath-stealing pants. *She's not dead.* Verda stopped short of asking a ten-year-old if he'd checked. She forced herself to inhale. Slow. It helped immensely in clearing the remnants of the nightmare in which she'd been trapped. She stepped aside. "All right," she said. "Come in. Sit next to the fire where it's warm." Verda turned to Lizzie, her insides begging her to do something with the babe. Verda took up the poker and stoked the embers and tossed on a small log.

"Might I hold him?" Lizzie asked Noah.

To Verda's astonishment, Noah turned him over without the slightest hesitation, then swiped at the tears on his face with his sleeve.

Julius quieted momentarily and Verda took advantage. "We must see to Mrs. Lyall, Noah. I"—she drew in a deep breath—"I'll check on Mrs. Lyall," she forced herself to say. "You wake your uncle. We shall know more of what we are up against at that time."

"What about my Julius?"

"You can trust him with Lizzie." She glanced at her maid, who nodded.

"He'll be safe with me, sir," Lizzie assured Noah.

Verda mouthed her thanks and headed to the door to await her charge. This time, his hesitation was acute, but he leaned in and kissed the top of his brother's head then hurried to follow.

They hastened from her chamber in the east portion of the castle toward the main wing together until they reached the stairs that led up to the nursery and schoolroom. "I'll see you upstairs momentarily," she told him before dashing up without looking back.

Please, don't be dead. The closer to the third floor, the more her feet dragged. But thinking of the baby's cries had her running up the last few steps and through the corridor to the open doors.

The first one was obviously Noah's.

She stopped just inside the second one. The wet nurse lay sprawled across her bed, strands of her gun-metal hair sprouting from its long, gnarly braid. Her mouth was agape and her arms outstretched. Verda couldn't detect the slightest movement. *Oh, God. She* was *dead.*

Every instinct to run surged through her. Swallowing hard, she quelled the desire to dash from the chamber screaming and forced herself to edge closer to the body, where she was hit with the overpowering stench of whiskey. An icy river soaked her bare feet and she glanced down. The culprit was an upturned bottle.

A massive snore startled Verda into a jump. She splayed her hand over her heart, then, disgusted, shook her head and tapped the woman's arm. "Mrs. Lyall. Mrs. Lyall."

"Don't bother."

Again Verda jumped, this time her head jerking back and smacking the hard line of Mr. Oshea's jaw.

"Damn it."

Verda spun around, her own braid flying, smacking his cheek. "Blast it. Quit sneaking up on me!"

GOD. MARRY THIS *woman.* The recurring thought reared its head and seemed to be the only thing Sander could think of even if it meant suffering a broken jaw at every turn. She must have been freezing in that thin wrapper she wore. The sharp points of her nipples revealed a story, giving way to his own tale that had him tightening the belt of his banyan. He snagged the long tail of her glowing hair before it could hit the candle to start a different, less satisfying fire and tugged her into him.

Every soft body part of her molded to him. He drew in a deep, scented breath of powdery violets and nearly groaned. The fragrance dispelled the notion of winter pelting the castle with its torrential rain and the frigid waves crashing against the jagged rocks below.

"Mr. O-Oshea, please—"

Please? He started to lower his head.

"Mrs. Lyall," she gasped with a breathless wonder. Or, perhaps not, based on the hands pressing against his chest. "Master Noah." She finally shoved, jarring him from his lunacy. "The baby, Mr. Oshea."

Right. The baby. "Did you try to awaken her?"

She folded her arms over her chest. The look she shot him suggested he should be castrated and she'd gladly wield the knife.

"Of course you did."

She turned back, facing the bed. "Even if we were to wake her now, she's clearly too soused to feed an infant. The poor child would end up as drunk as her." She strode to the door and rubbed her... bare feet. "Where are your shoes?"

She shook her head. "I'll find Mrs. Knagg. She may have some idea of how to proceed with this disaster. Where is Master Noah?"

"In your chamber with your maid and Julius."

She nodded and hurried out.

Sander let out his long-held groan.

It echoed back as if he were in a valley—until he realized the rebounding sound was that of the semi-conscious wet nurse. He brought up his head where she mirrored his motion.

"Good morning, Mrs. Lyall," he said pleasantly.

"T'ain't mornin', is it, sir?" She rose on one elbow with her free hand going to her forehead.

"Shall I call for a tincture, ma'am?"

She stilled and, slowly, the current situation seemed to dawn on her. Her gaze met his.

"Is this a typical occurrence?" he asked her.

"Wot?"

"Don't play coy with me, Mrs. Lyall. Never mind. We shall find another solution for Julius. You are hereby relieved of your duties. A carriage will be waiting for you at eight this morning. I'll send a footman up for your... trunk at that time."

"You can't sack me." Her indignation came too late.

"I beg to differ, madam."

"You'll regret this. That infant needs me."

"I daresay cow's milk is more useful than you." Sander stalked to the door then turned back. "Shall I send a maid to help you pack?"

The sneer on her broad face belied the meekness in her voice. "No, sir."

He nodded. "Good. I suggest you be on time. Otherwise, you'll find your return trip much lighter than that upon your arrival."

Her mouth gaped open, shut, then open.

"Let me explain. If you are not in front of the door by the specified time with your belongings, they shall be left behind. Am I clear?"

Her mouth compressed shut.

"Excellent. I'll have an envelope waiting with your wages, though in all fairness, it would be my brother's right to forego any compensation due, as I'm sure you are aware." He left and made his way to the east wing to speak with Noah.

He sincerely hoped Miss Fairclough and Mrs. Knagg stumbled on a solution to keep Julius fed.

CHAPTER ELEVEN

Mrs. Knagg was a godsend. It was a phrase—truth—Verda would utter until her dying day. Her insides quaked uncontrollably, but no one seemed to notice because the elderly housekeeper had just entered Verda's chamber holding a small glass cylinder filled with what she assumed was milk. It looked like milk. Watery milk.

Julius's cries had worn down to simpering. But his little body shook with tired hiccups that broke Verda's heart.

Noah's lips quivered and his eyes held a suspicious glimmer, yet not a drop slipped free.

Verda wasn't sure what was going on with herself because her own eyes couldn't seem to focus very well.

Noah cuddled Julius to his chest. "I'll do it, Mrs. Knagg."

Mrs. Knagg moved to stand in front of him. "You're too small. Give 'im over, Noah."

The young master proved too stubborn, and his bottom lip took on a mulish line. "No."

Verda studied the glass in her gnarled hand. "What is that thing atop the cylinder, Mrs. Knagg?"

"It's a spout. Ain't got no nipple. There's prob'ly one in the stall. We'll worry on that tomorrow."

"The stall?"

"Where they keep the goats an' 'orses. Now, 'and over that child, Master Noah."

"No."

A standoff ensued that had Julius's cries gaining new momentum. It was Mrs. Knagg who let out the sigh of defeat. "Aw'right, you little bug—er, lemme show ye how this works." She settled on the settee next to Noah. "Hold 'im jus' so, up, so's some gits in 'is lil' tummy." She moved the spout to Julius's quivering lips.

Verda did not see how this could work. Noah was huge in spirit but so much smaller in physical ability. She shocked herself by moving forward. "Would you like me t-to try?"

Noah's lips trembled almost as violently as Julius's, but after a long, trying moment, the ten-year-old boy whom one could mistake for a mother figure nodded slowly. One of those tears of his slipped free even as he lifted his precious Julius to her own shaking hands. Only he had to show her how to hold him with both arms and how to support his head as if she were the child and not Noah. The baby was just so tiny.

Shockingly, Julius suffered through it all unfailingly. As if he could tell someone different held him and was uncertain in how to handle the fact.

"That's it, miss. Hold 'im up now." Mrs. Knagg set the spout to the babe's mouth and he suckled as if he'd been deprived of milk for days on end. "Careful, now, young Julius. Easy. Easy. Don' take too much too fast."

Mrs. Knagg rose and moved away, leaving Noah to quickly slide into her place. "You're doing real well, Miss Fairclough. I think my Julius likes you."

The tension in her arms was the only thing holding the baby in place.

"We need to release the air in his stomach. Isn't that right, Mrs. Knagg?" Noah said.

"*What?*" Verda wondered if she would ever *not* feel this sense of impending doom that had taken over her normally well-ordered life, picturing a teeny Julius flat on his back with her pushing on his little stomach until he'd deflated to the depth of a rose petal.

"I'll do it," Noah said, taking Julius from her. He laid the baby over his shoulder, thankfully, with Mrs. Knagg's close physical supervision. "See, Miss Fairclough? There's nothing to it." He patted Julius's back.

Sure enough, Julius let out a less-than-gentle belch and with, what appeared to be, half the milk of what he'd just consumed.

Noah jumped up with an "auuuck," still holding Julius.

"What the devil's going on here?"

All eyes turned to the growl from the open door.

Verda now saw what she hadn't noticed in Mrs. Lyall's chamber: the powerful shoulders filling a black silk banyan, his bare calves, and black slippers that covered large feet.

For all of a second, silence ensued. Then…

Julius sucked in a sharp breath and let out a heralding cry that could shatter the windows.

Mrs. Knagg jumped.

Noah gasped and dropped the baby into Verda's lap. She instinctively clutched him with her hand to keep him from rolling to the floor.

"That is quite enough, Mr. Oshea. There is no need to howl like a lion." Her comment stopped both Noah and Mr. Oshea, slowly pinning her with their too similar, cynically amused eyes that matched the storm clouds hovering over a churning sea.

"Lions don't howl, Miss Fairclough." The gentleness of Noah's tone contrasting with the messy contents Julius had cast all over his nightshirt left her disoriented.

Heat infused her skin from her bare toes to her cheeks in a raging inferno. "No, they don't, do they? A wolf howls, and I vow that is what I am about to do." She spoke firmly. Pointedly. "You all seem to have forgotten this is *my* chamber."

She speared her gaze on Noah. "You! Change your nightshirt. And bring whatever clothing the babe needs." She turned to Mrs. Knagg. "Prepare another concoction so we shall have something in the event of an emergency. Lizzie, accompany her to the kitchens and bring it back to save Mrs. Knagg the trouble." She frowned. "Julius has cast up most of what he'd downed in the first place."

Saving her most scathing scold for last, she met Mr. Oshea's fired-up gaze with one of her own. "You, sir"—she pointed—"will cease your dictatorial manner while standing, inappropriately, I might add, in my bedchamber." It was suddenly all too much. The backs of her eyes stung. She was shockingly and dangerously close to tears. The last time she'd cried had been when she'd been eight years old. This was unacceptable.

She dropped her gaze to Julius and picked him up—he'd fallen asleep—laying his head on her shoulder, as she'd seen Noah do. Each small maneuver gave her confidence, the lift she needed. "Master Noah, you and Master Julius shall sleep the rest of the night in my chamber. You are all excused."

Noah hurried past Mr. Oshea and Mrs. Knagg with Mrs. Knagg and Lizzie right on his heels, leaving Verda to face the lion all alone in her own den.

She was tired, she was scared, and worst of all, she was attracted to this very real threat of a man. The Rathbournes of the world she could handle. "I thought I excused you, sir." She couldn't decide if that tone in her voice sounded wary, petulant, or peevish. Peevish seemed the most appropriate option.

"I see you've overcome your fear of infants. I had no idea when I hired you as a governess for Noah that you possessed nursemaid skills as well." Amusement poured from him that she did not find so amusing.

Besides, she had not overcome her fear. Not really. They went deeper than he could ever imagine. "You've no idea the things I've defeated," she bit out. Julius stirred and she heaved in a deep breath to remain calm. It seemed the child resonated with the slightest effusion of emotion. "It's late."

"Yes." The single, soft-spoken word raised the fine hairs on her arms and at her nape. The man meandered closer, sending her body into a jumble of conflicting palpitations. And Julius into a wriggling mass nearly sliding off her shoulder. Mr. Oshea's large hand came up and steadied him before taking hold of him completely.

He cradled Julius in the crook of his arm, then pierced her with eyes that had taken on the gloomy darkness of the chamber.

Verda stood and took the two steps to the fire, absorbing its warmth, because the temptation in Mr. Oshea's gaze was much too tempting. "You shouldn't be here. What will people think?"

He surveyed the chamber, before settling his gaze back on her. "What people?"

"You know what I mean."

"I don't care what people think," he said with sudden seriousness. A seemingly deeper significance to his words vibrated through her.

Hugging herself, she rubbed her upper arms. Of course he didn't. "I don't suppose you do. Men don't contend with the same stigma imposed on women." Her gaze was drawn to the now-quiet Julius. "Why aren't his eyes gray? From what I've noticed all of the Osheas, men and boys, eyes are gray."

He tipped the child and studied him. "Both Lucius and Noah had eyes the same color as infants. I believe they change to their permanent color within the first year."

"How odd." How content the baby appeared. So content, Verda found herself wondering if those arms of his uncle's were large and strong enough to calm the rioting flutters surging through her. "What is to be done with Mrs. Lyall?"

"She will be departing first thing this morning."

"That is best, I suppose. But what of Master Julius? He must have nourishment. Infants do not eat like... like regular people. At least I don't believe they do."

He smiled. "No, they do not. I'm certain other children have survived without a mother's milk and he will as well."

Verda wasn't so sure. Many babies died within their first year. Her eyes fell on him and blurred a little. Just those few moments of holding him had changed something innate within her. Her arms tingled.

"Do you worry something will happen to him, then?"

"Of course. Didn't you see Master Noah's nightshirt? He likely failed to retain anything in his tiny stomach." She shivered.

Mr. Oshea smiled down at the babe. "He seems content enough to me."

She stole another look. That was true enough. A streak of warmth pierced the constant ice that always seemed prevalent within her lately. She couldn't tear her gaze from the tranquil Julius.

"That look on your face." Mr. Oshea spoke softly. "It's most... entrancing."

Slowly, Verda lifted her eyes, meeting his. As if she couldn't have, based on the lure in his voice.

"If I didn't have my hands full..."

But he did. "If you didn't?" Oh, lord. What the devil was she saying?

Noah burst through the open door clutching Julius's basket. "I'm back," he announced on a breathless rush. He slid to a stop in front of Verda. "Where's my Julius?"

She took him by the shoulders and turned him to face his uncle.

"Oh. Shall I take him now, Uncle Sander? He might require changing."

"Indeed, Noah," he said with a smile in Verda's direction.

Noah dropped the basket and stepped forward to take his brother. "Miss Fairclough, all his changes are in the basket. Take them out and I'll show you how..."

"Er, Noah, I'm not sure—"

Mr. Oshea did the deed himself while Verda watched, fascinated, at the complicated business of pinning a napkin in place. Mostly, her eyes were on Mr. Oshea and his handling of the situation.

Moments later, Lizzie returned with the glass cylinder full and topped with the spout.

"Noah," Mr. Oshea said as Noah rose from placing Julius in the basket, still fast asleep.

"Yes, Uncle Sander?"

"You will allow Miss Fairclough to hold Julius when it's time for him to eat. Is that understood?"

"But—" Verda started.

He speared her with that dark look. "Or I shall find myself sleeping this night before the fire myself. Am I clear on this?"

His words had her swallowing any retort.

She knew he wasn't speaking just to Noah, though his attention remained on his nephew.

"Yes, sir."

"Excellent, Noah. I shall find you more blankets, after which I will leave you all to your much needed rest."

As if she'd rest after a threat of him sleeping in her chamber.

SANDER SAUNTERED OUT of Miss Fairclough's chamber. His chest swelled with warmth that spread through to his limbs, fingertips to toes. Seconds later, a grin split his face and his thoughts ran amok. God, that hair of hers would drive him wild. The softened look in her eyes when he cradled Julius… She would make an excellent mother. Her instincts were quite sound. Her fears… What was it she feared?

She hadn't killed her father like he had. The man still lived and breathed to wreak havoc on her life. Sander wanted nothing more than to wipe the worry from her face with kisses. Her forehead, her eyes, her lips.

He wanted to marry her but was it fair to subject her to a life with him, without her knowing the secrets he carried?

He pushed that train of thought out of his head and wandered the massive hall.

Where the devil did one find extra blankets in this monstrosity of a hovel?

✦━━━━✦━━━❖━━━✦━━━━✦

CHAPTER TWELVE

T HE NEXT MORNING, Sander woke early and dressed, wondering how the governess and her charges had fared through the night. As tempting as it was to storm the corridors to her chamber, he resisted. Instead, he ordered a morning repast sent to her chambers in his stead.

He took his place at the table in the morning room, where it was much warmer. A dated copy of *The London Times* lay next to his plate and he opened it, accepting coffee from Hicks. It was strong and hearty, emboldening him for the day ahead.

The door swung wide and Damien entered as if he hadn't up and disappeared the last week. "Why is the carriage on the sweep? Did you already frighten our maiden and ill-dressed governess into leaving? What the devil possesses her to wear such horrid, drab colors..."

Annoyance spilled through Sander and he glared at his brother. "As a matter of fact, the carriage is for the wet nurse you hired."

Damien's hand went up, signaling Hicks, who hurried over with another cup. "What's wrong with her?"

"She's a sot. Noah couldn't wake her last night for Julius's feeding."

"Julius? Oh, the infant. Bring me some eggs," he barked at the footman.

"Christ, Damien. He's your son." Sander compressed his lips, withholding a rare temper. Once he had his emotions under tight rein, he cleared his throat. "Where have you been?"

"Roaming. What do you care?"

"You missed a meeting with the governess." That was a ridiculous thing to bring up. He hadn't wanted to remind him of Verda.

"Ah. How *is* that lustrous wife of yours?"

Not quite mine yet. "Doing well. Noah appears to like her very much." *As do I.*

"Good. Perhaps he'll quit harassing me about attending school with Lucius."

"Perhaps," Sander murmured.

"Can't believe the child isn't dead yet," Damien went on.

Shock reverberated through Sander, leaving him momentarily speechless. Hatred, even. Blood roared in his ears that rivaled the pounding in his chest. "How can you say such a thing?"

Damien leaned back in his chair, an elbow on the arm and leaning casually to one side, staring at Sander through a calculating squint. "Is he? Just like I was father's son?"

The pain in his brother's voice was barely discernable, yet it seemed to bound against the horrid portraits lining the walls. The sting wasn't limited to Damien. It stole through Sander's blood like poison. His insides constricted as if he'd ingested a handful of bitter horse chestnuts. "What are you saying?" he choked out.

Damien glanced at the footmen. "Get out," he barked. He waited for the men to retreat. "I know that I was not sired by Father's seed. *You* are the rightful heir."

"This, again? I am not. You are and you have two sons to follow in your steps."

Damien was suddenly leaning forward, his hand a hard pound on the table, sloshing coffee from their cups. "Quit lying to me," he bit out. "I know the truth. I've known it for years." He drew in a deep breath and let it out in a long, slow stream.

"That changes nothing." Sander lowered his voice, but the words came out through a locked jaw.

Damien fell back against his chair once more. "I suppose that is true."

Sander gave up all pretense of eating. "How did you learn?"

The devil's own smile fleeted his brother's expression. "Father blurted it out just before he bloodied my nose—"

The statement heralded Sander back to 1810. He'd been sixteen at the time, Damien a year older.

"Father's a bastard. You should run away." Damien's indignance on Sander's behalf touched him.

He shoved a handkerchief in Damien's hand. "I can't." Though his greatest desire was to join the fight against Napoleon on the Peninsula, every day, Father grew more deranged and uncontrollable. Sander dared not leave Damien to their father's wrath. Father would kill Damien just as soon as look at him.

What a blackguard their father was. No matter the past, Damien was the Pender estate's future.

Sander's build and coloring was more like Father's, whereas Damien was slighter and more elegant, taking after their mother.

Damien couldn't quite hide a shudder that shook his shoulders, further sinking Sander's hopes for escape. Damien's hands clenched and unclenched at his sides. "You're an idiot," he said with only the scantest tremor to his voice.

"Idiot or not, I'm not leaving." The chances of Sander ever seeing his brother alive again if Sander were to abandon him was a real threat. "We leave together or we stay together."

They locked eyes for a long moment, until Damien blinked. "All right, it's your neck."

And yours. But Sander bit the inside of his cheek. "Where's Father now?"

"Hell if I know. Taking the long walk off the scantest cliff, I hope." Damien turned away.

It pained Sander to see his brother so... so tormented. He reached out to take his arm, but Damien shoved him away with a bloodied hand, leaving a wide streak to stain his shirtsleeves.

Fury surged through Sander: at his father for treating Damien so harshly, and Damien for his sudden rejection. At only a year apart, there had never been a time they hadn't had one another's backs. "Where's

Father?" he demanded.

Damien tore up the stairs two at a time without looking back. "How the bloody hell should I know? Leave me be."

The rage tearing through Sander was both abrupt and precipitous with nowhere to go.

The door blew back and the swirling wind appeared a life of its own, and within its midst, his father but a blackened silhouette. The man stepped into the low-light of the sconces. One hand wrapped a leather strip.

Father stopped, his eyes drawn to the dark streak along Sander's arm. "Where is he?" he growled.

Sander put his arm at his back while stepping away from the seething violence that mingled with the swirling wind. Fear gripped him by the throat and he shook his head.

Father started to the staircase.

"Outside," he said quickly. "I-I don't know where. H-He was upset, said something about the cliffs."

"Bastard." Father spun on his booted heel and disappeared into the blinding, blowing blizzard ravaging the Northumberland night.

"You remember, the night *you* sent him to his death." Damien laughed, a maniacal ripple that turned the morning room into a medieval torture chamber, complete with the winds howling and branches rapping the windows.

"Yes." Sander rose from the table, went to the windows, and shoved his hands in his pockets. He stood looking out at low, black clouds and dark skies that were all too common in his nightmares. "Yes. I remember."

VERDA'S HAND, POISED to push the latch, letting her into the morning room, froze, two things slamming into her fogged brain: the missing earl had returned, and Mr. Oshea had killed his father.

The gloom in the corridor grew sinister. In the space of seconds, a long clock's pendulum ticked loudly, seeming to scrape against her throat. If she didn't move, she would collapse to the floor in a pool of her own blood. Cobwebs would fall from the rafters to suffocate her. It took considerable effort to drag her mind from the self-debilitating fancies she'd concocted.

The accusation lobbed at Mr. Oshea from his brother should have terrified her. Had her running to gather her own trunk to accompany Mrs. Lyall from this castle of horror.

Instead, a surge of empathy encased her heart. She had no desire to see Mr. Oshea embarrassed or humiliated. She, more than anyone, knew the heaviness of a loved one's death at one's hands. The fear, the guilt. The questions pounding through one's head. *What if this had been done differently? What if that hadn't happened? What if she'd been older—*

Her head jerked back, rejecting the awful recollections.

She forced herself to breathe. Twice. Then, slowly, she backed from the door without entering, then hurried to the servants' stairs for the kitchens to speak with Mrs. Knagg directly, regarding Julius's feeding and care now that Mrs. Lyall had been relieved of duties vital to the babe's very life.

Noah and Julius were now her most urgent undertaking, though grimly, she had to acknowledge that protecting her virtue was as well now that the Earl of Pender had since returned.

Alas, that wasn't the most frightening aspect. It was her own attraction toward Mr. Oshea that posed her the greatest threat. A threat that could only lead to ruin.

DAMIEN LET OUT an impatient huff. "Your martyrdom grows tiresome. You didn't kill Father, Sander. It's true you sent him over the moors. But it was to protect *me*. As much as that grates, he deserved what he got. It's years past, besides."

Sander didn't turn from the windows. "I'm not looking for absolution. I know what I did."

"Then what are you looking for?"

A question that plagued him every night when he crawled into his cold and lonely bed. *Her.* He wanted Verda Fairclough. She enticed him to an absurd degree. But how could he offer for her when he had sent his own sire to his death? He couldn't bear witnessing the censure, the accusations, the disgust that would surely follow.

"Now, about our new and enticing nursemaid—" Damien's drawl, dripping with sarcasm, penetrated Sander's despondence, sending a shock of black waves of rage coursing through him.

In an instant, he had hold of his brother's neckcloth and was yanking him to his feet without any recollection of having crossed the room. "She was not engaged for her services as a nursemaid. And certainly not to provide you with entertainment," he ground out. It was a tyrant of a move, as Sander stood a head taller than his brother and weighed a good two stone more.

Intimidated? Of course not. Damien laughed, sending not just shivers, but raw fury snaking up Sander's spine, squeezing each vertebrae. Damien shoved him away.

Astonished and appalled at his own loss of control, Sander dropped his hold. "Leave her be, Damien, or rest assured, I shall kill you, just as I did Father." He shoved him away.

Damien's eyes narrowed as he dropped back into his chair. "I'm unused to threats." His voice was a low growl that didn't discompose Sander in the least. "Especially those issued by you." Genuine amusement curled his lips, as if mocking Sander. It only served to infuriate him to the point of doing his brother great bodily harm.

Damien shoved away from the table. "Now, if you'll excuse me, I believe it's time I met with the lovely Miss Fairclough." He sauntered out.

⁂

CHAPTER THIRTEEN

So, THINGS HAD come full circle—to Verda's great dismay. She stood outside the earl's study, just as she had a week prior. Only this time it wasn't with trepidation but irritation that set her teeth on edge. The man was a menace to his family, from his brother to the baby Julius. Any previous intimidation from the Earl of Pender had long since plummeted.

With a deep inhalation, she rapped firmly on the oak door.

"Enter."

"My lord." She injected the same tone she used with her own father. The pragmatic, straightforward voice that brooked no tolerance for tomfoolery.

His practiced scrutiny crawled over her, leaving a vile film of repulsion in its wake. She shuddered.

"Is there some reason behind the drab finery?" he said, inclining his head at her brown, woolen frock.

"I'm a governess, my lord, not a debutante awaiting an approach from the Wall of Wallflowers."

"Well played," he murmured. "Please, be seated."

Verda took the chair and waited.

"I understand the wet nurse drank herself into a stupor and has been relieved of her duties."

"Yes."

"My brother says you've stepped up admirably to the position of nursemaid."

His tone scraped her skin raw, but she kept her temper in

check. "Perhaps. But the wet nurse served in a way that was unique only to her."

His eyes dropped to her modest bosom before rising to meet her gaze. The cynical twist to his lips sent hot waves of embarrassment washing over her along with a healthy dose of outrage. She jumped from her chair and flattened her palms on his desk. "You, my lord, *will* do something about another wet nurse for your son. I am *not* at your disposal." She couldn't stop there. No, her temper was an unforgiveable flaw in Papa's eyes, and words were her weapons. "Perhaps you should locate another governess as well. Master Noah is a bright lad who deserves more than rotting in this pile of rubble." She stifled a groan and chastised herself for never knowing when to stop, always digging the hole deeper. What she should tell him was that the pile of rubble needed updating. But, no. She maintained the reserve that she used with Papa and hoped that would suffice.

Surprise flitted over his face accompanied by a bark of laughter. He recovered quickly enough with a short cough and a wave of his hand. "Sit down. Sit down."

She straightened and backed from the desk.

"You've nothing to fear from me. Sadly," he added, though it sounded as an afterthought.

Lips compressed, she studied him for a long moment, then slowly lowered into the chair. "As long as we are clear, my lord."

"Oh, yes, we are definitely clear. My brother has already threatened to kill me."

"*Kill* you!" she blurted out, startled.

"Aye," he said with some impatience. "Might we move on?" He let out a long sigh. "I wish to know more regarding Noah and his interactions with the infant."

"Julius?"

"Er, yes. Julius, you say?"

She was incredulous. "You don't even *know his name?*" She stood up, prepared for her escape. "It's obvious someone responsible must stay near those children. They require protection. Where is Mr. Oshea? He, at least, shows some attachment to their care. You, my lord, are an abomination."

"As I keep telling my brother." The degenerate earl's expression never even cracked.

One could deal with only so much stupidity. Verda swept from the study, desperate for a sudden breath of cold air. Anything that could pry the guardian knot lodged in her throat.

SANDER STROLLED INTO the study. "Set you in your place, did she?" Truly, Miss Fairclough was the woman of his dreams.

Damien's scowl lightened the tightness banding Sander's chest. "I thought you'd given up listening at doors years ago."

"Ah, well. How else am I to learn the things I need to know to protect those I care for?"

"Like how I wasn't of Father's blood?" Damien's fingers clenched into fists atop a short stack of papers.

A sore subject, but perhaps needed a clearing of the air. "Yes. Like that." Sander had heard their mother's deathbed confession to their father that Damien was not of their father's blood. He'd been six. It was then he'd realized he was the only one who'd protect his brother despite being too young to understand the whys. "Do you have other questions?"

A smirk crossed Damien's lips. "Plenty, but they shall keep. Your woman rightly pointed out that the wet nurse was uniquely qualified for her position."

Sander barely heard the last half of his brother's statement, leaving him stuck on the "your woman." They lodged in his chest like a woodsman's axe. He ran a tingling finger around the neck of his shirt, tempted to tear away his simply tied cravat and toss it in the grate.

Damien cleared his throat, and it penetrated.

The earl pinched the bridge of his nose, then pierced Sander with a rare solemnity. "You didn't kill Father," he said.

The statement struck through Sander like a bolt of lightning out of a stark blue, calm, and definitely, tumultuous-free sky.

"It's true, you sent him into the freezing weather on a wild grouse chase," he went on. "Hell, if he'd ever deigned to listen to me, I would have done the same."

"I don't know what you're talking about," Sander said on a huff of impatience.

"I'm trying to explain something here. And I'll only say so once." His hand waved out. "I witnessed your entire exchange with Father from the floor above that night. He was drunk. As usual. He'd cornered me in the stables. Blasted me with his usual diatribe. That particular night, his accusations centered around sabotaging the horses."

Sander fell into the closest chair, certain his legs wouldn't support him much longer. "I didn't know." He hardly recognized the low huskiness of his own voice.

"He held a leather strap, was tapping it against his hand." Damien's eyes lost their focus to a past scene. "I screamed at him." He blinked and was back in the present, but there was a tremor in his hands. "He told him when I addressed him, I would show respect." One hand squeezed into a fist.

"As if you hadn't always treated him thus." Disgust bordered the hatred broiling Sander's blood. "That's when he hit you."

"Yes. But I shoved him back. Knocked him out. I thought *I'd* killed him. Baldric appeared like the ghost he was. Sent me scrambling inside to find you."

"I know all of this, Damien. What I don't know is—"

Damien held out his palm, his jaw as taut as a violin string. "I'm not finished. What you don't know is that *I* followed him that blustery night. *You* didn't *kill* him."

Sander froze. "Are you telling me that you…"

"No. And that is the end of the conversation. Neither of us offed the scoundrel. Much as he deserved it," he finished on a mutter.

A flush of heat started mid torso and crept up like an unsolicited guest, leaving Sander at a loss as to do with this sudden shift of a past he'd always believed. He stared at his brother.

Damien flexed his hand. "The subject is now closed."

Sander willed back his question. This was as open as he could ever recall since their childhood. He drew in a deep breath. "Right, then. To the business at hand. What *are* you going to do about the children? Should Miss Fairclough remove herself to London"—something Sander would do his utmost to prevent—"Noah will have nothing to occupy that overdeveloped brain of his."

"Not quite true. He has the infant." Ire colored Damien's tone and raised the pressure in Sander's blood. "Which is enough to keep anyone busy."

The thoughtless remarks had Sander rubbing the spot between his eyes. "His name is Julius, Damien. And while that may well be, it is short-sighted thinking. Noah confessed to the lady he wishes to build a laboratory. Without her supervision, he's likely to turn this place into the mound of rocks it deserves. Unfortunately, he and Julius would likely be buried beneath the rubbish. I doubt you would find that a desirable outcome. I could be wrong, of course," he added somewhat spitefully.

"Right, as always," he bit out. "That is not a desirable outcome. Perhaps it is I who should build the laboratory. You can take the children to London—better yet, Cornwall."

"Dear God. Listen to yourself," he said on an exasperated huff. "Perlsea Keep is in worse shape than Stonemare." A violent storm in 1755 had nearly wiped it off the cliff. "The place is barely sustaining itself. If you continue on this current path of gambling losses, the Pender fortune, such that it is, will be gone within a fortnight."

"That is a gross exaggeration."

"Is it? Have *you* ventured a look at the books?"

Damien's lips tightened.

"Of course you haven't. The fact of the matter is, we must

move out of the Bronze Age to more modern methods of sustaining our heritage. The cottage industry is a dying means for the villagers, backbreaking and unsustainable. More specifically, Lucius, Noah, and Julius's heritage is at stake." Sander breathed in deeply. "But I digress. We must locate a new wet nurse, first and foremost. The need is quite urgent."

"How do you propose I do that? That is woman's business."

Sander was not above using guilt to push his points home. "Well, it is now your business. Mrs. Knagg is handling the kitchens and the gardens. We have few enough servants for all the tasks she is undertaking due to the ridiculous beliefs that Stonemare is haunted and how no one wishes to serve here." All true, though it was not due to funds. It was due to isolation. Even the neighboring viscount spent little time in this barren, almost forgotten portion of England.

Damien winced, which Sander found reassuring. At least his brother still harbored human compassion, even if it was but a thread. "And if there's not a wet nurse available?"

"Noah cannot care for an infant by himself," he said gently. "At the least, we shall require a nursemaid."

"Miss Fairclough—"

"—was hired as a governess. Not a nursemaid," Sander said smoothly. "Now, I suggest you start composing correspondence. Address it to the general merchant in Alnmouth. 'Tis a hub of information."

Chapter Fourteen

Three Weeks Later

V ERDA PACED HER maid's chamber she had taken for her own since seeing the reptiles in her bed as if she were a nocturnal ghost. The long clock's chime of three had woken her. Quite telling for two reasons: one, she shouldn't have heard only three chimes in the first place, considering how distant her chamber was compared to the others, and two, had she been asleep…

Therein lay the crux. She hadn't been sleeping. Caring for an infant even with said infant's caretaker had left her spent. The treks up to the schoolroom level at all hours of the night assuring herself the two were well were taking their toll.

Three weeks. It had been three blasted weeks before Lord Pender and Mr. Oshea had finally announced Lord Pender would be taking the carriage the next morning into Alnmouth to pick up Julius's new wet nurse.

This macabre castle was straight out of the Middle Ages and was freezing, making it impossible to get warm. Snow clung to the metal strips of the mullioned windows and was still pouring from the sky with a melancholy wind adding to its haunting enigma. The curtains, so threadbare, did nothing to keep out the cold, so she stoked the fire to a blaze. With freezing fingers, she went to a chest of drawers where Lizzie had unpacked her own unmentionables. She dug out a pair of woolen stockings and pulled them on.

Even donning her heaviest wrapper did nothing to ease her restlessness. She went through the sitting room door to her own chamber and peered in where Lizzie slept as soundly as a contented cat in the huge bed.

Verda's walk earlier that day had been cut short due to the unrelenting rain and winds. She was in the most deserted portion of the castle, wasn't she? Who was there to see if she did a quick turnabout and back that was sure to stir her circulation. She lit a candle, because she wasn't a complete idiot, and exited to the corridor by way of the sitting room.

Shadows flickered like long-boned fingers against the walls. She closed the door behind her to retain the heat. Just a quick march to the portrait gallery and back. *You can do this*, she told herself.

Halfway to her destination, she heard a voice.

"What the hell do you think you're doing?"

Her own gasp extinguished the light after she'd caught only his demonic eyes. Terror rippled over her and she backed away. Her arm was snagged in the dark, tugged against a warm, hard chest, lips captured—

The instinct to struggle was immediate until the tip of his tongue touched the seam of her lips and she dropped her candle.

"Blast it," he groaned against her lips. "That's my foot."

Mr. Oshea, *not Lord Pender*. At her gasp, his tongue entered her mouth and stroked hers. Her lips molded against his. Called home to a bright summer morning. A meadow dotted with grazing sheep and fresh grass covered in dew and a colorful array of flowers in every shade of rainbow hues. Blues that filled her spirit, playful pinks, cheerful yellows, and deep reds that stirred a passion she'd never guessed she possessed.

This wasn't her. Clandestine meetings with a man she barely knew and may have killed his father. *Secrets*. She pulled away yet still clutched his arms in an iron grip. "Mr. Oshea?" She should have been indignant. Outraged. Not this breathy heroine with no brain in her head like those she imagined in Mrs. Radcliffe's novels. Somehow, her fingers edged up and found their way to the nape of his neck and touched the silky strands of his hair.

"Miss Fairclough?" Noah appeared, holding his own candle and the baby. "It's my Julius. He's hungry, ma'am."

Verda jumped away from Mr. Oshea—guilt, shame, not remorse or regret. *Oh, lord.* She didn't need the Duke of Rathbourne or the Earl of Pender to humiliate her. She was making a fine hash of the situation without anyone's assistance. "Of course, Master Noah." Her voice quivered with self-condemnation. "I'll take him. Run and get the cylinder."

"One moment, Noah." Mr. Oshea had picked up her candle and he lit it from his nephew's. "Hurry now," he said a second later.

The little master pierced her with a perception beyond his years. The insightful look lasted but a second before he dashed for the stairs.

Verda laid the crying infant against her shoulder and followed Mr. Oshea back to her sitting room. She lowered to the settee while Mr. Oshea stirred the embers in the hearth and added more fuel.

"What the devil were you doing prowling about?" Mr. Oshea demanded.

"I-I couldn't sleep. I-I thought if I did a quick walk, it would help."

Julius's cries grew stronger.

She met Mr. Oshea's eyes. "We have to do something to help him," she said. "I can't bear it when he cries."

"Why couldn't you sleep?"

"I'm worried."

"About?"

"Little Julius, Master Noah, I don't know." *You.*

He took the baby from her and rocked him.

"This is getting to be a habit," she said more tersely than she'd intended. She pointed at him. "You… You *kissed* me."

"And it was quite delicious. I'd like to do it again." The look he slid over her had her wanting to throw the windows wide to breathe since his presence seemed to suck the oxygen from the chamber. "But next time, I want all that hair unconfined."

He was the absolute devil.

She narrowed her own gaze. "And what were you doing in this wing?"

"Making certain you were safe, of course." He let out a sigh. "Miss Fairclough, until three weeks ago, you were terrified of holding Julius. We still don't have a wet nurse. Nor a nursemaid. Forgive my bluntness, but your lack of confidence when it comes to an infant does not leave me inspired."

Her shoulders fell. She had no argument for that. "What a dreadful thing to say. I thought I was handling the situation moderately well." How devastating that he could be right on all accounts. She would make a horrible nursemaid, let alone a mother.

SANDER CONSIDERED RECANTING his words at the dejection written in Miss Fairclough's face. But he couldn't very well tell her his brother had disappeared from his bedchamber and Sander hadn't been able to find him. Appointing himself as her personal guard was all well and good, but telling her might terrify her into rushing back to London on the first mail coach in the height of winter. It was true. He did not believe his brother would assault a woman against her will, but... what if spirits were involved? A man not in full control of his faculties represented risk. And how was he to convince her to marry him if she feared his brother?

He opened his mouth to reassure her she was safe from the earl, but Noah hurled through the door. "Here it is, Miss Fairclough. I have it."

Verda rose from the settee and moved within smelling distance of Sander. He swallowed another groan just as he was once more inundated with the distinct fragrance of powdered violets. It was just so out of place in the musty confines of Stonemare.

He handed off Julius and she returned to the settee. Noah clamored up beside her, cylinder in hand.

Sander knew he should leave, but his head refused his commands to obey and he took up the wingback chair and watched her. A dark broodiness went through his body from his toes up.

"You're getting really good at feeding my Julius, ma'am," Noah said.

"Thank you, Noah. It's very nice of you to say"—she sent a pointed gaze at Sander—"as my lack of confidence fails to inspire some individuals."

"Not me," Noah said with great enthusiasm.

After situating Julius on her lap, she took the cylinder from her greatest champion, smiling at him. "No, not you."

CHAPTER FIFTEEN

VERDA STOOD IN the foyer still fatigued from her nighttime visit of nephews and uncle. Mr. Oshea and the earl were leaving for Alnmouth and she could hardly wait to fall into bed anticipating a full night's sleep… but what if the woman the earl had hired didn't understand Julius? What if she insisted Noah's assistance was a hindrance? What if…

Enough, she berated herself. She stopped just short of banging her forehead against the nearest wall. Mostly, due to Lord Pender's presence.

Mr. Oshea appeared and descended the stairs. "I fear Mrs. Lyall had the right of it when she said she was the only wet nurse in the region," he said, whipping his greatcoat around his shoulders.

The statement made no sense to her. "That seems quite unlikely, doesn't it? I mean babies are born fairly often." Then added because she wasn't quite sure. "Aren't they?"

"A sorry business all around," Lord Pender growled.

Verda restrained an eyeroll.

"I suspect it's Stonemare," Mr. Oshea said with a grim smile. "It has a reputation."

She snorted. "You mean that business of it being haunted?"

Lord Pender grinned. "Don't forget 'lurid.'"

A look of irritation crossed Mr. Oshea's features and he appeared to ignore his brother and looked to Verda. "Where did you hear that?"

"From Mr. Colbert. He told me to call him 'Cracked.'"

A burst of sharp laughter rent the air. Lord Pender's. "Colbert's cracked all right."

Mr. Oshea shook his head. He fastened his coat at the neck and plopped a fur-lined hat on his head. "We shall return."

"Bye, Papa. Bye, Uncle Sander." Noah lifted Julius's hand and flopped it in a wave from the door of the library with all the confidence of an aged nursemaid.

Verda set a hand on Noah's shoulder as doubts flooded her. "Are you certain this woman is necessary?"

"You don't miss your privacy, Miss Fairclough? Of course, she's necessary." Lord Pender's tone, she was learning, was more bark than actual bite, though his arrogance was vastly annoying.

Mr. Oshea met her gaze. "You and Noah cannot be expected to manage the constant care of an infant."

True. It was a miracle Verda could function at all. "Very well. Travel safely, sir, my lord. We shall see you when you return."

Verda tugged Noah and the baby into the room and out of the vestibule and the ancient front door's draft.

The heavy door clanged shut after them and the silence left her oddly bereft.

Three weeks of adapting to Julius's erratic schedule had indeed exhausted her. She was looking forward to a full night's sleep. She didn't know how Noah coped so well. Youth, she supposed. "Shall we attempt Greek and Latin today?" she asked her charge.

Noah let out a groan reminiscent of his uncle.

She hid her smile and led him to the settee so Noah could place Julius snuggly in his basket near the hearth. She'd used this time each day to visit with Noah. Coax his aspirations from him outside of taking on Julius's care.

Mrs. Knagg had already supplied a tray of tea for her, chocolate for Noah, and a cylinder of watered-down goat's milk they'd taken to feeding Julius.

Selecting primers from a stack on the table, she went to the settee and set them on the space beside her, poured herself a cup of tea with a dash of milk, then settled back. Before she could pose a question, Noah blindsided her with his own.

"Are you going to marry Uncle Sander?"

Verda somehow managed not to send tea spewing over her serviceable brown gown. "B-Beg pardon?" Her gaze was caught in the innocent and unblinking stare he leveled on her. "Why on earth would you ask such a thing?" It took a minute before she managed to break the eye contact to fumble with refilling her cup instead. With shaking fingers and verve, she finally cut a side glance to him.

"You kissed him," he accused her. "In the dark."

"My, er, candle blew out." An appallingly weak counter.

"That doesn't make one kiss," he smartly pointed out.

No. That was a side benefit. Verda closed her eyes. She couldn't very well say that. "Are you certain you saw a kiss?" Proving she would make an excellent candidate for Bedlam.

Again, she was hit with his amusement, so cynical for one so young. How long would it take Julius to perfect that expression? She doubted she would be around long enough to learn. A depressing thought.

"All right," she acknowledged on a hiss. "But you will never mention this topic again. *He* kissed *me.*"

Noah's brows furrowed. "What's the difference?"

Nothing, based on her reaction at the time. She'd enthusiastically responded, clung to those broad shoulders. Stunned, that she hadn't been frightened in the least. Any thought of being cold? Sizzled away with the heat of his lips and his hands. "Something you shall learn as you grow older. Now"—she picked up one of the primers and tossed it in his lap—"shall we start with Latin?"

He lifted the book with a smirk, once more reminding her of his uncle. "Sure. But this is Greek."

TWO GRUELING HOURS with Noah left Verda tempted to snatch her hair out. But Julius woke, finally putting her out of her misery with a need for changing and feeding. She handled the feeding portion then turned the infant over to Noah's care and donned her coat for a brisk walk.

A quick glance at the hovering clouds showed the rain at bay, if just barely. She found her normal path in a biting wind that whipped her skirts into a frenzy. The cold piercing her lungs was welcome, loosening the constricting tightness. She made her way through a copse of trees and was rewarded with droplets of cold rain sliding along the back of her neck beneath her cloak. The path through the trees opened up along the cliffs, but she was cognizant of Mr. Oshea's voice in her head, warning her of the wind.

Indeed, it was strong enough to knock her off her feet. The crashing waves below deafened her and she reveled in the isolation of the moors and the vast sky. She raised her face and arms to the heavens, welcoming the gusts that dampened her face with a light mist.

Verda heaved in several bracing breaths before lowering her arms. It was time to return. She turned and headed back to the copse and froze, tilted her head, and listened.

"Help." It was faint. It was female. It was young.

"I'm here," Verda called. "Where are you?"

A shaking voice led her off the path farther into the trees.

More drops saturated her bonnet and cloak, and worse yet, the rain began its torrent from the clouds. The trees acted as a leaky umbrella, protecting her some, but clearly, she was running out of light. She followed the voice to a dark lump taking cover between a fallen log and a low-branched tree.

Verda ran to the girl and lowered to her knees.

The child's hair was darkened by the rain and plastered to her head, her eyes puffy from crying. "Oh, thank goodness," she cried.

"What happened? Are you hurt?"

"I twisted my ankle, I think."

"Where do you live? How did you come to be on Pender land? What is your name? What are you doing out here *alone?*" Verda barely restrained herself from taking the girl by the arms and shaking her. Instead, she sucked in another, less calming breath.

She stared at Verda with wide dark eyes, her mouth slightly parted.

"My apologies. Perhaps we should start with your name?"

"Lady Docia Hale. I-I live at the neighboring property to the north."

"All right. Do you mind if I check your ankle?"

She shook her head and Verda ran her fingers over the girl's left ankle, which was somewhat swollen. "How did you get here?"

"I rode my pony. I fell off and she ran home." Lady Docia sniffed back more tears and swiped her nose with her sleeve. "At least I hope she ran home."

"How old are you?"

"Eleven."

Verda smiled. "Too big for me to carry, I fear. Let's get you to your feet. I'm afraid you'll have to return with me to Stonemare."

"I don't mind," she said. "Ghosts don't scare me."

Verda came to her feet and, bracing herself, helped Lady Docia to hers, but the instant the girl put the slightest amount on her left foot, she nearly toppled back to her bum but for Verda's hold on her. "Whoa there."

Verda slipped an arm beneath the girl's and slowly, they made their way to the path and through the small forest.

The overfilled clouds let loose their deluge, making for a most uncomfortable trek to Stonemare. Once they'd reached the edge of their meager covering, Verda was dismayed to find the carriage parked in the sweep. "Oh, dear," she murmured.

"What?"

Verda didn't have time to answer.

Mr. Oshea emerged from the portico. Verda couldn't read his expression, but there was no hiding the determined gait of his forward motion and in the swing of his arms. He was furious. The rain was a transparent shield that would do nothing to save her.

She waited on the perimeter of the forest because she couldn't very well run and leave the girl to her fate.

When he was just close enough, Verda called out. "We're here."

He shifted direction at her voice, sending a shot of relief through her. "What the devil are you—" Mr. Oshea stopped. "Lady Docia?"

"She's hurt. Her horse threw her and ran home. I happened upon her," Verda said in a rush.

His jaw tightened. "I'll carry her. Run to the house."

Verda nodded and dashed for the portico, her cloak no match for the maelstrom. By the time she'd reached the open door and stepped into the foyer, she was soaked and frozen to the bone, her teeth chattering. She didn't abandon her post, however. "Mrs. Knagg, towels, please."

Mrs. Knagg nodded and hurried away.

Seconds later, Mr. Oshea entered the hall. The young girl he carried was beautiful and would be extraordinary in another few years.

"Why were you riding your horse in this weather? You know how dangerous the moors are?" Mr. Oshea was chastising her. Verda followed them into the library. He set her down gently. "Does your father know what you were about?"

Her eyes flashed with fury, but she quickly lowered them and picked at her skirt.

Verda shot him a glare. She went to the girl and assisted her with her sopping cloak with shaking fingers that were so cold, they were numb.

"I'll do it," Mr. Oshea said brusquely, pushing her icy hands aside.

Mrs. Knagg entered and Verda took the stack of towels from her.

"You best bring tea," she told the woman, then turned to the girl. "Are you hungry, Docia?"

"It's *Lady* Docia. My papa is a viscount." She smoothed her gloved hands over the skirts she'd picked at. "Yes. I'm famished."

Ah. A little empress solidly aware of her station in life. Almost. While Verda was a mere baron's daughter, and she had rarely attended social events, it was common knowledge that a viscount's daughter was addressed as a 'miss.' The fact that no one corrected her was confusing at best, but now was not the time for such questions. "My pardons, *Lady* Docia. It is my pleasure to make your acquaintance, my lady. I am Miss Fairclough. Master Noah's governess."

"The pleasure is mine," the little peeress returned primly.

Verda hid a grin.

The tenacious Mr. Oshea cleared his throat. "I asked you a question, young lady."

"And, you—" He pointed at Verda, his chest puffed out with the deep breath he'd inhaled.

She braced herself for the coming annihilation but couldn't quite suppress her chattering teeth.

Just as quickly as he'd breathed in, his chest deflated with a sound exhale. "Go. You'll catch your death. We shall talk later."

Verda threw her shoulders back, lifted her chin, and strolled out as if she were queen, despite the chill coating her skin.

Thunder roared outside that could hardly be heard over the heavy rain lashing the windows.

CHAPTER SIXTEEN

ONCE AGAIN, SANDER was on the wrong end of the continuum when it came to preserving his usually tranquil temperament. Miss Docia Hale, the viscount's daughter, as she so blithely informed them, huddled beneath a blanket near the fire. He wanted to shake her for putting Verda in danger—herself as well. He had a few words for the absent viscount.

Damien strolled into the library. "Miss Bash has been turned over to—" He stopped, having caught sight of Docia. His head tilted to one side, then he shot Sander a look, his brows raised.

"*Lady* Docia fell off her horse and twisted her ankle," Sander said without an ounce of inflection in his voice.

"I see." Damien strolled to the hearth. "And what were you doing riding on such a day, my dear?"

She didn't meet his gaze. "I wanted to see Lucius."

"Lucius is at school," Damien returned. "You knew that. He left months ago. Does your father know where you are?"

"Papa's in London."

"And your sister? Apologies, I've forgotten her name."

"Eleanor. She's dead."

"*Dead.*" Sander hadn't heard that.

Damien winced. "Ah, I'd forgotten that as well. Well, you aren't staying at Chaston all alone. Who is in charge of looking after you?"

"My lady's maid, Olive. I was hiding from her. She hit me and I ran away."

"What of your governess? Surely, Chaston didn't fail on that duty?"

Funny question from Damien when Sander was constantly forced in reminding him of his duty to his own sons.

"That's why he left for London," she said. Her feet didn't touch the floor—they gently swung crossed at the ankles. *Ankle*. He peered closer. The right was crossed over the left, the one she'd supposedly twisted.

With a glance out the windows, Damien let out a sigh. "You'll stay here tonight," he told her. "The weather's too dangerous to return you to Chaston." He addressed Sander. "Send Fletcher over with a note that Miss Hale will return tomorrow."

Sander noted the little miss hadn't bothered correcting Damien, though her face tightened expressing her displeasure. For as long as Sander could recall, the entirety of Alnmouth had indulged Docia as a child who appeared to have a father who, upon the death of his wife, had forgotten his children. A tragic situation all the way round. He strolled to a small escritoire and penned the missive then pulled a chord for the footman. After dispatching the note, he moved to the seating area and took the wingback chair. "I'm sorry for your loss," he told her.

Eyes downcast, she lifted one shoulder. A second later, a lone tear splashed on her leather kid glove.

He rose from his chair and held out his hand. "Come along, Lady Docia. Let's find you a chamber and get you warmed up before dinner."

She raised her gaze, taking his hand to stand, and gave him a brilliant smile. "Thank you, sir."

Sander led her from the library, leaving his brother, who rose and went straight to the brandy. He pulled the door closed behind them and indicated she precede him on the stairs. "What made you believe Lucius was home?"

"Oh, he didn't want anything to do with school," she said emphatically. "I believe it's due to talk of Lady Pender's having a child and then her death. I was certain Lucius would be back for that."

"The earl opted not to bring him home. The weather is too erratic this time of year."

Her composure was impressive. "I thought it certain he would run away from school. We're to marry, you see."

Sander choked out a cough. "Pardon?" He narrowed his gaze on her, but hers was on her feet, her skirts in a dainty hold between her fingers. "He is only thirteen, Docia. This is not the Middle Ages, where women of nobility marry at the age of twelve." Not to mention the little matter of that contract Damien had signed with Rathbourne regarding the duke's daughter. A fact Sander chose not to voice.

She came to a stop, frowning. "It's *Lady* Docia, and I'm eleven."

Hiding a grin, Sander nudged her into motion. "Well, you've plenty of time to work things out. I expect Lucius will return home in a few months. Noah is in residence. He is looking after his new brother. Perhaps he can keep you company."

"I don't much care for Noah," she said.

Sander managed to keep from rolling his eyes. "This way, my lady."

CHAPTER SEVENTEEN

VERDA SAT BEFORE the hearth in her chamber and ran her fingers through her newly cleaned hair. Her feet were encased in warm, woolen stockings and she wore her heaviest brown frock. As tempted as she was to crawl into bed, she had yet to meet Miss Bash, Julius's new nursemaid.

It was not her place to approve of the woman, she reminded herself, but Julius was an infant.

Also true, Noah would pitch a scandalous fit if he found the woman lacking, but Verda wished to confirm the woman's capability herself and as exhausted as she was, she would never rest well not knowing.

She had Lizzie braid her hair and loop the ends properly off her nape in the event she happened into, say, er, Mr. Oshea.

Outside her cozy chamber, the castle could have been encased in ice. Her toes too, but for her thick stockings. Her sensible shoes echoed on the uncarpeted floors and the wooden steps up to the schoolroom level.

Julius's cries reached her before her feet hit the third floor. She took off in a run.

"What's wrong?" she demanded on a breathless rush of air.

Noah stood in front of a young woman whose dark hair was pulled tight at her nape. She couldn't have been fourteen—younger than Verda had expected—holding Julius. And with a full bosom that nearly spilled from her not-so-serviceable gown.

Noah had his hands planted on his hips and was leaning forward in an aggressive stance. "She doesn't know how to hold him."

Miss Bash looked as if she were about to cry.

Verda took in the situation. "Master Noah, I implore you to take a deep breath."

He didn't.

She went to him and placed her hand on his shoulder. "In the event you've forgotten, you had to show me how to hold Master Julius as well."

"But—"

"No," she said, sternly cutting him off. "You must afford Miss Bash the opportunities you allowed me. I insist. Now, breathe, please."

He sucked in a deep breath and let it out, though not as slow and steady as she would have preferred.

"Thank you. I would like a moment with Miss Bash. Wait for me in your chamber. In fact, I believe a Lady Docia Hale is around somewhere. You may visit with her."

"Docia!" He stomped to the door. "I'll wait in my chamber for you. Alone."

She let out a sigh. "Fine. Then I shall speak with you shortly. Close the door on your way out."

With a scowl on his face, Noah did as she'd bidden.

Verda turned to Miss Bash. "Would you like me to hold Master Julius for a minute?"

"Thank you, miss," she said, handing him over. "I-I was unprepared for his brother's attack."

"Yes, he's quite protective." Verda gave her a small smile. "Their mother died in childbirth as I understand it."

Her expression softened. "I'd heard, of course." She looked toward the door. Her eyes flickered. "I don't believe any of that nonsense that the castle's haunted. No matter what the people in the village say."

Her words momentarily distracted Verda. "The townspeople believe—never mind." She laid Julius over her shoulder and patted his back, which instantly soothed him. "I'm relieved you are so sensible. The place is daunting, but I've yet to run into ghosts." She studied the girl. "Is this your first position as a nursemaid, Miss Bash, Maura... Do you mind if I call you 'Maura'?"

She shook her head, "Maura is quite all right, miss." Her teeth grabbed her bottom lip. "If you don't count my five younger siblings—"

Verda stopped her. "Um, how old are you, dear?"

"Twenty-two," she said to Verda's shock. Maura let out a sigh. "Mama didn't want me to leave, but Papa..." Her voice trailed off.

"Your papa?"

"I shouldn't say, but, well, we need the blunt, and he quite insisted."

Verda suspected her 'papa' resembled her own in many ways when it came to funds, and of course, did not do much in the way of assisting with the younger children. Disgust rippled over her. *Men.* But then an image of Julius in Mr. Oshea's capable hold materialized in her head.

Maura strolled to a small table and picked up Julius's cylinder. "Master Noah thrust this at me and said Master Julius needed to eat. As you can see, he hasn't." She stared at the bottle. "There is no wet nurse, is there?"

Verda winced. "No, the wet nurse was a sot. Master Noah couldn't wake her for a night feeding and Mr. Oshea dismissed her. She was dispatched the next morning. You don't imbibe, do you?" The horrified look on the nursemaid's face reassured Verda. "Never mind. I was jesting."

Julius let out a hiccup that Verda realized could quickly escalate into a full-blown fit.

"Why don't you try feeding him?" she suggested. "I'll wait here with you."

"A-All right," Maura said softly, hesitantly.

"We'll try a non-moving chair to start with before the rocker.

It will feel more stable," Verda instructed. Maura sat down and Verda placed Julius in her arms. "Master Noah must have laughed his fool head off when he showed me how to hold him. I have no experience with children, you see."

"You've never married?" She sounded so horrified, Verda laughed.

"No. Much to my own papa's consternation. Nor, have I ever before been a governess. I much prefer my independence. Settle him in your arms. Then I'll hand you the cylinder. He's really quite sweet."

After a moment, Verda handed her the cylinder and watched as Maura concentrated on working the nipple of the cylinder in Julius's mouth. "He is, isn't he?" It finally took and Maura smoothed a hand over his fuzzy head, a tiny smile curving her lips.

Verda watched Julius gobble down the watery goat's milk so she could report the progress to Master Noah. "If you don't mind a bit of advice…"

Maura glanced up. "Of course, ma'am."

"I would recommend allowing Master Noah to assist you. The child knows his brother. And he truly is a great help."

"I will. Thank you," Maura said on a rush.

"Now, I best move along to placate, er, reassure him." Verda left the hungry Julius into the sweet care of Maura Bash and walked the two doors down to Noah's chamber.

He was pacing like a feral cat until he spotted her in the arch.

"You didn't bring him?" Goodness, another two seconds and he would have been fit for Bedlam. Something to which she could easily relate.

"He's fine, Master Noah."

"He cried the second I handed him over."

"And once you left the room, he calmed down."

The familiar mulishness firmed his lips.

Verda moved into the room and took a small, wooden chair. He stormed by her, but she caught his hand, stopping him.

"Darling, it's very difficult to share something or someone so precious, but you want the best care for your brother, don't you? If something were to happen to you, heaven forbid, who would be there to look after him?"

He was quiet for a long time before his shoulders dropped and a suspicious sheen glistened his eyes. "Nothing will happen to me."

"Likely not. But there are no guarantees. And you will be leaving for school in a few years." She paused. "Remember how frightened I was to hold him?"

He gave her a reluctant nod.

"But the second you dropped him in my lap, I learned that he would not break. I implore you to think beyond yourself and think of Master Julius. I believe Miss Bash will make a wonderful nursemaid for your brother, given half a chance."

The stubbornness remained, but after an interminable time, his little chest caved in. "I suppose she is not so far from the ancient days."

Verda let out a shocked cough. "Er, no, I suppose not. She is younger than I."

"You're not old," he said magnanimously.

"Am I not?" she asked with mock worry.

"No." With every word, he came more into himself. "Papa and Uncle Sander are much older than you. I suppose I can give Miss Bash a chance." His fists landed at his hips again. "But she'd better not drop him."

"I don't think you have to worry," she assured him. "Now, about Miss—*Lady* Docia…"

CHAPTER EIGHTEEN

THE LIBRARY WAS the warmest chamber in Stonemare, Verda decided, as did every other inhabitant, save Maura, who'd remained in the nursery with Julius. The rain, momentarily abated, preserved a chill that penetrated Verda's heavy, woolen dress of olive to her skin.

"But I don't wish to go home." *Lady* Docia Hale, it appeared, possessed the privileged capacity to evoke tears on demand.

Verda would have been convinced, too, had she not just heard the girl needling Noah for his "nursemaid" tendencies. She'd bristled with outrage on his behalf. Thankfully, he'd restrained from launching himself at Docia. Her curiosity heightened to see just how far the girl was willing to take this latest act stage-worthy of the Theatre Royal in Covent Garden.

"Why not, dear?" This was the earl, showing a side of—not compassion, exactly—interest, perhaps. At the least, his cynicism was not on its usual full display.

Her bottom lip trembled just so. "There's no one there." The tears descended Docia's cheeks. Big, fat drops made a slow trek when she blinked those eyes of startling azure, framed by long, now spiky, lashes.

Verda restrained from rolling her own.

"I shall drive her home," Mr. Oshea said. "Miss Fairclough, perhaps you won't mind accompanying us?"

She instantly agreed, as she could use a much needed escape from the castle's oppressive atmosphere. "Certainly."

Noah gave Verda a disgusted look and stomped out of the chamber without a word.

"I doubt the rain will be held off long," Mr. Oshea said. "We should leave immediately."

Verda nodded, frustrated, as there was no time to reassure Noah, vowing to speak with him upon their return.

THE ROAD TO Chaston was fraught with ruts and mud that rattled the brains. Verda held on to the strap for dear life. From the corner of her eye, Verda admired Docia's composure. It exceeded that of any young ladies she had ever encountered, though that wasn't saying much, as she'd never had the privilege of children's company.

Neither did Mr. Oshea appear off-balance in the least, with arms folded across his chest, legs splayed to keep him centered, and, annoyingly, stealing all the breathable air in the confined space.

"I hadn't heard your sister had expired, my lady," he said. "You have my abject condolences."

"Thank you, sir," she said sweetly.

"She was young, was she not?"

Her gaze turned out the window. "Sixteen."

"That is indeed young."

"Will I have to stay at Chaston? I'm haunted by her memory." Her voice was soft, pitifully so.

Guilt pelted Verda for her uncharitable thoughts. There was just something about the girl that set her on edge. Perhaps she was projecting Noah's prejudices. Still, Docia had been unmerciful in her taunts to him regarding Julius. Julius couldn't be a more fortunate babe with such a staunch caretaker. And Verda would defend Noah's choices to the death.

She turned her gaze out the window to the raging storm,

releasing a sigh. It took near an hour to reach Chaston and her relief was monumental. Her bum was certainly thankful.

The carriage stopped close to the portico.

Mr. Oshea didn't wait for the steps to be laid, whipping the door back himself and jumping out.

Docia's expression was one of horror.

Verda took her arm and pushed her to the opening. "Hurry, my lady."

Mr. Oshea's arms proved as capable with an eleven-year-old girl as with a month-old infant. He handed her off to Fletcher and held his hands out for Verda.

"Truly?" she asked.

"Don't tell me you're frightened." Plops of rain hit his grinning face. "You have a wish for wallowing in the muck, do you?" With a sharp, wolfish grin, he snatched her by the waist and set her under the portico then followed her inside the Chaston manor house.

They were met at the door by a young woman with dark hair secured at her nape. Her gray eyes were wide and worried. "Oh, Miss Docia, you're back. I fretted all night. We received the note from Lord Pender..." Her eyes went to Mr. Oshea and her voice trailed off.

"How many times must I tell you, Olive, it's *Lady* Docia."

She flinched under Docia's sharpness and gushed. "Of course, of course." She dipped a shallow curtsy. Her eyes crept back to Mr. Oshea. "You are—" She gulped loudly. "Lord Pender?"

Verda tried to see Mr. Oshea through Olive's perspective. He and his brother had the same shade of eyes, the same dark hair, but there the differences ended—to her. It was in the wrinkles creased at the outer corner of his eyes and mouth, indicating his outlook on life that was not so dire as the earl's view.

"No, my dear, I am his brother, Lysander Oshea," he announced with a bow, forcing Verda into hiding a grin. He turned to Verda. "It was Miss Fairclough here who found your mistress on the moors with a twisted ankle."

Olive gasped. Between the two of them, they could turn a handy profit in treading the boards, Verda decided. "Twisted ankle. Oh, my lady. Are you quite all right now? I didn't notice you limping." Quite the observation, now that Olive had mentioned it—Verda hadn't, either. It appeared the lady was quite recovered.

"Your papa had to leave for London." Olive spoke on a rush of sheer exuberance.

Annoyance covered Docia's pretty features. "Of course, he did, Olive. He's bringing a governess. Now, please inform Mrs. Garrett we are in need of refreshments."

"But—"

"Now, Olive. The weather is quite frigid. Hurry along."

Verda had trouble reconciling the girl's manner coming out of such a small body with the child's voice. It was a fascinating study that titillated through her similar to that of reading Elizabeth Fulhame's chemistry experiments. She couldn't turn away.

Mr. Oshea stopped the maid. "One moment, Olive."

"Sir?"

"How many servants currently reside in house?"

"Mrs. Garrett, she's the housekeeper. Cook, and me. Oh, the stablemaster, but he doesn't sleep in the manor."

Mr. Oshea turned to Docia. "Where is all your staff?"

Her slippered toe dug in the carpet and twisted back and forth. "They've just been leaving. Especially since..." Her voice trailed off and she shrugged.

Since what? Verda's eyes snapped from Mr. Oshea to Miss Docia. Verda had only met her the afternoon before. A confident child who'd seemed confident in her position. Even embellishing herself from 'miss' to 'lady.' What she saw now was a child whose shoulders had fallen, whose chest was deflated. A lonely, forlorn little girl with very few servants around.

She saw *herself.*

Mr. Oshea's jaw tightened. "Did Lord Chaston indicate how

long he'd be gone?" He spoke through clenched teeth.

"H-He left a note for… Miss—Lady Docia."

"Might I see it, please?"

"Um…" She cast an unblinking glance to Docia, who shrugged. Then she dashed from the drawing room. Seconds later, she was back holding a piece of vellum.

He read it in silence, his brows furrowing.

"I see." Mr. Oshea turned to Docia. "All right, my lady. Pack a bag. You must return with us to Stonemare."

"Oh, thank you, sir. Thank you." She ran and threw herself into his arms. The childlike behavior appeared genuine and caught Verda by surprise. And, if she were being honest, warmed her inside.

Mr. Oshea's arms tightened slightly around her before setting her back on her feet. "Hurry now."

"I'm not sure—" Olive started.

"I'm going, Olive. You may stay here if you so choose." Miss Docia dashed from the room.

An odd expression crossed her maid's face, but it was as unreadable as it was fleeting. She turned and followed her charge.

A long moment ensued while Verda stared at the door. "That is a very nice thing you did, sir," she said softly.

"We couldn't very leave her here alone with only a cook, housekeeper, and lady's maid."

Verda smiled. "Don't forget the stableman."

"Indeed." He smiled too.

With that minute exchange, the shell Verda had vowed to keep sternly in place, the one encasing her heart, fractured. The lesion was tiny, but the sound reverberated in her ears, discharging pulsing flecks of light. The sensations confused the pragmatic logic she lived her life by.

The difficulty to breathe was only due to the constricting corset. That was all.

Willing back the desire to place the back of her hand to her forehead and call for a vinaigrette, she took slow, shallow breaths until her vision cleared. She then patched the small fragment in her chest through sheer force. And logic.

SANDER STOOD AT the windows with his hands in his pockets. The rain hadn't let up and if they didn't leave soon, they could very well be stuck. He watched Verda's reflection on the glass, never turning his head. Something was wrong. He wheeled about to see her face pale then flush. Alarm skittered through him. He was at her side in an instant. "What is it? Are you ill?"

"I-I'm fine." She pushed away from him, stepping back. "Of course, you couldn't very well leave her here with just three other women. But it's odd that neither Stonemare nor Chaston are able to keep servants. Certainly Chaston isn't considered haunted?" she said lightly.

His hands fell slowly to his sides. "No." The touch of amusement in her voice assured him she was all right. Perhaps the low light was playing havoc with his senses where she was concerned.

She smiled, though it appeared to tremble. "As difficult as it is to fathom, she is a child." She shook her head. "What on earth would possess her father to take for London in such a squall? Surely, the need for a governess could have waited until a more opportune time?"

Sander moved to the table he'd set the note upon. He picked it up then strolled to her and held it out.

Her head tilted and her eyes questioned him. She reached for it and read it as he had. Silently. She raised those lovely eyes to his. "I don't understand. It reads as if a… a child penned this."

"My exact thought. I suspect the viscount has been gone longer than her maid let on. I have no choice but to bring her to Stonemare."

"Yes." A long breath escaped her. "It won't be that difficult to include her with Master Noah's lessons." She turned a stern look on him. "But I warn you, I fail miserably at embroidery."

"I suspect she could instruct you in the art," he teased. The issue released another fragile split.

She spun on her heel, putting her back to him, and setting the note back on the table. "Bite your tongue, if you don't wish to send me after Lord Chaston in the same horrid weather." He wasn't certain, but it did sound as if she spoke through some obstruction.

He glanced back toward the windows. The panes rattled in response to the hammering gales. "I must speak with Mrs. Garrett. I don't suppose you wouldn't mind—"

VERDA STRODE TO the door. "I'll see if I can prod the lady herself into action."

She took the stairs to a third level, not because she knew where Miss Docia's chamber was, but because her father owned a country house and children were typically assigned to the third level and the servants the level above that.

The layout of the house was pleasant compared to Stonemare with its cold halls and worn tapestries and rugs. She followed voices down the corridor to the far end on silent feet due to the thick carpets.

"But I must go with you." Olive was quite insistent.

Miss Docia overrode her. "No. Lucius told me there are plenty of servants."

Verda held back a snort. From what she'd ascertained, the castle could have used another thirty outside the six to ten she'd observed to date.

"And if I insist?'

"You won't," Miss Docia said sweetly. "Now, hurry. I need my trunk. The weather's growing beastly."

Verda tapped on the doorframe, startling the both of them.

"I'm afraid Olive has the right of it, Lady Docia. There are fewer servants than Lucius let on about. I insist you accompany us to Stonemare, Olive. But the weather will play havoc on our trip back and we mustn't dally." She tugged on her governess status, spearing Miss Docia a stern look. "The carriage shall be departing in fifteen minutes with or without you."

Miss Docia's lips firmed in a way Verda was learning to associate with the age via Noah.

"I'll be there, Miss Fairclough."

"And your maid," Verda said.

Miss Docia shot Olive a lethal glare. "Fine."

"Thank you, Miss Fairclough." Olive's docile reply belied the look in her eyes. She was older than her charge by some five years, but it was quite clear it was Miss Docia who ruled. While usually the case, Verda acknowledged, the young lady could certainly stand lessons in ladylike behavior. Especially if she went about claiming to have the title of 'lady.'

"Shall I send Fletcher up for the baggage?"

"Yes, thank you," Miss Docia said.

Verda made her way back down the hallway, but the slamming of the door echoed behind her. Quite soundly, and she found herself swallowing back a shock of stunned laughter.

CHAPTER NINETEEN

S ANDER TOOK LITTLE comfort in the carriage on the way back to Stonemare, although the rutted roads did play in his favor in throwing Miss Fairclough almost on his lap a time or two. Until she wised up and grappled the strap, doing her utmost to lengthen the distance between them.

Even in the gloom, he detected her fiery blush—it glowed almost as bright as her hair—which was further deepened by the other two occupants sitting across from them. Already, he'd had to hide his amusement in keeping his gaze trained to the nearly visionless landscape.

The ride was tedious. For what should have taken thirty minutes had already stretched to over an hour. The coachman, Dermid, was due a raise if he managed the journey without a cracked wheel or axis. Fletcher as well just for having to ride beside him.

"How much longer?" Docia was not a patient young lady.

The trap opened and Fletcher's face appeared. "There's another carriage blocking the portico, sir. 'Fraid it'll be a soggy trek to the portico."

"Thank you, Fletcher. Have Dermid maneuver as close as he can," Sander said. The trap shut and he addressed Docia. "To answer your question, we're close. Bundle up."

"To whom does the other carriage belong?" Miss Fairclough murmured.

"Oh, it must be Lucius," Docia said. Excitement emanated

from her in her inability to sit still.

He barely heard her over the pelting rain, but the same question occurred to him.

Their own conveyance rolled to a stop, but Sander's ears still vibrated with the roar of the rain and rutted roads vibrating his head until he thought it would fall from his shoulders into the muck. Clearly, he would have to carry each of the occupants inside and he planned to save Miss Fairclough for last.

Docia was first. The lightest and quickest he dropped inside, where things were in chaos.

If Sander had been shipbound, Damien's voice could be heard over the crashing waves. "Do you realize the danger you've put the horses in, traveling in such conditions?"

Sander heard no response and hurried back out to bring in Docia's maid. "I'll return shortly," he told Miss Fairclough.

"Out of my sight, you little bastard. I can't bear to look at you." The harsh growl reverberated through the hall. *Damn* Damien. He hadn't an iota of sense. Any more than their sire had had.

He'd set Olive on her feet just as Lucius tore out of the study and pounded up the stairs, fists swinging at his sides. The boy's looks were identical to Damien's at Lucius's age of thirteen. Just what the devil was going on?

There was no time to find out now, however. Miss Fairclough couldn't very well sit in the carriage until he dealt with the issue. Drenched through, Sander stepped back out into the deluge. To his great disappointment, Dermid was moving the carriage to the portico due to Baldric's removal of the other now rounding the side of the castle in the direction of the stables.

Well, that was disappointing. He'd rather relished the idea of carrying the woman over the thresh—Gads, he was an idiot. With a sigh, he pulled the door back and leaned in with a grim smile. "It appears my nephew has indeed made his way home from Eton unexpectedly. The fireworks inside would give Vauxhall a run for blunt," he told her.

"Oh, dear. The earl's not pleased to see his son, then?"

"To put it mildly." Sander took her gloved hand. Its warmth reached through the soft kid leather and he held it a touch too long for propriety's sake. He met her emerald gaze that reflected the storm surrounding them. "We must hurry." Though he could have stood there all night into the next day. "There's no need for two of us being soaked to the gills."

Her hesitation was minute.

"I don't bite." He shot her a wolfish grin. "Not hard, at any rate."

Once more, that dash of scarlet heightened her cheekbones.

The opportunity… opportune. And who was he to resist? He tugged on her hand, startling her right into his arms.

Right where she belonged.

VERDA NEEDN'T HAVE worried that anyone would witness her in Mr. Oshea's arms. The entryway was devoid of even Mr. Winfield. Couldn't Mr. Oshea have held her a tad longer? He assisted her with her cloak, his fingers brushing her nape, raising the fine hairs there. He, of course, was soaked… to the gills. "You'll catch your death," she said on a breathless rush.

"Likely so. I shall have to change before I am up to dealing with the current crisis," he told her. He took her by the shoulders and gently pushed her in the direction of the library. "Warm yourself by the fire. I shan't be long."

Mrs. Knagg entered from the back of the house. "Oh, thank be to the heav'ns, yer back. I'll bring you tea. The girl and 'er maid's awaitin' as well. The girl's a'cryin' 'er eyes out, she is," she blustered out before hurrying away.

Verda contained her groan, straightened her spine, and marched into the library. The nice, warm library.

Docia and Olive were near the fire with their heads together, whispering.

Verda moved in front of them. "Is everything all right?"

"Um, of course." Docia lifted her gaze and blinked. One fresh tear trekked down her cheek.

"Obviously, something is wrong, dear. What is it?"

She gave a delicate sniff, so perfectly ladylike. "Lord Pender yelled at Lucius. He showed no restraint for decorum. He told Lucius to get"—she hiccupped—"out of his sight. He called him a… a bastard," she finished on a whisper. "That's n-not t-true, is it?"

"I've been trying to explain to her ladyship," Olive said in a low voice with an awed glance to the door, "that just because someone is called such a thing doesn't make it so. The earl was very angry."

"I'm certain all will look different in the morning," Verda assured them, not at all certain.

Unshed tears pooled. "But, is he really a… a…"

"Docia," Verda said firmly. "He is Lord Pender's heir."

"Yes." She took a lace handkerchief from a small reticule, Verda hadn't noticed before now and dabbed at her pert nose. "He's a viscount. Perlsea."

"Thank you. Lord Perlsea is certainly not a bastard. It sounds as if the earl just lost his temper a bit." *Unsurprisingly.*

"It's *Lady* Docia," she corrected through a sniffle.

Verda clasped her hands at her lower back. "Apologies. Another point of fact, *Lady* Docia, is this is a family matter." She kept her tone soft—mostly. "And, frankly, it is none of our concern."

Mrs. Knagg, thankfully, entered that instant where the fragrance of scones fresh from the ovens hit Verda's nose. Her knees almost buckled from hunger. She sank in the nearest chair and quickly poured out three cups of tea being as there was no lady of the house, and deliberately handed the first one to Olive.

A huff of irritation emitted from Miss Docia.

Verda then selected a scone for the maid and handed that to her too. "Olive," she said so sweetly, her teeth ached. "Would you allow your mistress and me a moment of privacy?" She pointed to the table she and Noah used for his mathematic lessons.

Olive shot Docia a quick glance, though the girl didn't acknowledge her in the least.

"We'll only be a moment," Verda added. "Now, please."

"Of course, miss."

Once Olive had moved across the room, Verda offered Docia a scone. "How do you prefer your tea?"

"Four sugars and milk." The excessiveness was not unexpected.

Verda handed it over, then doctored her own with just milk. She leaned in and lowered her voice. "Treating one's servants without respect reflects poorly on oneself, my dear. You should have a care."

Miss Docia's eyes filled with those unshed tears that glistened into pools of midnight. As always, the suddenness stunned Verda. The girl, too, leaned forward. The move sent another perfectly dropped tear down her face. "But, Miss Fairclough, I fear for my well-being. She's quite horrid to me when no one is about."

Verda's insides stilled. Her eyes cut to Olive and back. "That's a little difficult to fathom. I've seen no evidence of such action."

"But it's true," she said in all earnestness. She set her cup and plate aside and pulled her sleeve back, revealing a dark bruise on the inside of her wrist.

"If that is indeed the case, why didn't you say anything to Mr. Oshea—or me—before now?"

"I tried telling you in my way. You just refused to listen. Besides, Papa would be livid had I left her behind. He said she is to go everywhere with me. H-He made me promise." The tears flowed freely now.

Doubts plagued Verda. It had been Olive who'd insisted on accompanying Docia. Not the other way around. Verda grabbed a serviette and placed it in Miss Docia's hand. Hadn't her own father demanded the same when Verda had been young? *Actually, no.* The only lady's maid Verda had ever had was Lizzie, who a few years back had been released, then reinstated when Papa had decided she was to set her cap for the Duke of Rathbourne. Not to mention, Docia was an eleven-year-old child. Their situations were entirely different. "All right, dear. Dry your tears. Crying doesn't help." She sat back against her chair, still studying the girl.

"But—" Verda followed Docia's eyes to where Olive maintained a docile pose at the table. Her black hair blended into the mourning drapery behind her, displaying her face in stark paleness, her gray eyes nearly black.

"Docia—forgive me—*Lady* Docia, did Olive put the bruise on your wrist?" Verda asked. The girl's mouth opened, but Verda stayed her with her palm. "I want the truth."

Her head dropped. "No, ma'am. I fell."

Verda reclined back, letting out a long stream of air, and considered her next words carefully before leaning forward again. "Thank you for your honesty. That is the true definition of 'lady' to be sure."

Her gaze snapped up, as if she didn't believe what she'd heard.

"But I absolutely insist you treat her and others with more respect. That will only help you going forward. Do I make myself clear?"

"Yes, Miss Fairclough. Thank you. Thank you so much." She picked up her scone and took a small bite. "This is most delicious, isn't it?"

Verda narrowed her eyes on the girl, confused as ever.

CHAPTER TWENTY

O NCE SANDER HAD changed out of his saturated clothes, he made his way to the third level and down the corridor to Lucius's chamber. His thirteen-year-old nephew was sitting in a chair staring out the window. "Lucius?"

"Did you come to box my ears as well?" His sullen tone banded Sander's chest.

"Have I *ever* boxed your ears?" Sander returned.

"You're the only one who hasn't. It's a wonder I've not sustained a crack in my skull." His attention remained trained out at the powerful storm beyond.

"Is that why you're home? Did someone attempt to crack your skull, as you put it?" Sander's gut tightened at the thought. Lucius was highly sensitive. More so than Noah, who would take on the world for his infant brother.

Lucius rose from his seat, shrugging and not meeting Sander's eyes.

"How did you manage the journey home? It was quite expensive, was it not?"

Another shrug. "I won some decent wagers." He lifted a fiery gaze to Sander. "Why was I the one who had to leave? Noah's the one who likes learning. I know everything I need to know."

"This again?" Amusement mingled with exasperation seeped beneath Sander's skin. "You think so? What of your Grand Tour when the time comes? The friends you attain at Eton will be your friends for life."

"I don't have any friends. And I don't care."

"You may not care now, son, but someday, you might."

"I won't." He plopped back down in his chair, set his chin on his fist, and turned his gaze to the fire in the hearth.

There was a tap at the door and Noah strolled in, his constant companion's head lying on his shoulder. "Lucius? I heard you'd come home."

Lucius turned his head, eyes widening, interest flaring briefly. "Why are you tugging the brat about everywhere?"

"This is my Julius."

"That's a dumb name."

"It is not," Noah said hotly. "He's our brother."

Lucius's lips curled into a sneer reminiscent of Damien's. "Oh, that's right. He killed Mama."

"That's enough, Lucius," Sander snapped. "Your mother suffered horribly." It hit him quite suddenly why Lucius had made his way home. And in such horrendous weather. "Noah, Miss Fairclough is in the library. Perhaps you and Julius could keep her company."

Noah glared at Lucius and stormed from the chamber with Sander saving the door from slamming behind Noah's fierce departure.

"You're upset about your mother," Sander suggested softly.

Lucius jumped from his chair and faced Sander with his hands clenched into fists, his stance tense and leaning forward. A fighting position, to be sure. "Why should I care about *her?*"

Sander ticked off one finger. "She was your mother." Ticked off a second. "You didn't have an opportunity to say goodbye." Ticked off a third. "You loved her." He dropped his hand. "It's difficult losing one's mother, son." As Sander well knew. *The crunch of a harsh fist breaking delicate bones. The ensuing silence…* But Sander quickly pushed that memory right out of his head, or at least to the outer fringes. It was Lucius who needed his assistance now. His own nightmares were saved for the depths of night.

Lucius, blinking rapidly, turned away. "Why does Noah call

the baby 'my Julius'?" Only the smallest tremor in his voice betrayed the roiling emotion he was attempting to conceal.

Sander went to Lucius, placed his hands on his nephew's shoulders and squeezed. "He said your father gave Julius to him. I believe it was Noah who named him. Turns out he's quite the nursemaid—*and* I'll thank you to keep that sentiment to yourself."

Lucius shook off Sander's hold. He brought up an arm and swiped it across his face. "Least it's got his nose out of all those stupid books he reads all the time."

Sander smiled. "Not completely."

Lucius turned, having gotten control of himself, and faced Sander. "What do you mean?"

"I hired Miss Fairclough as his new governess. I expect you'll be joining your brother for lessons since the weather is too hazardous to return you to school."

Lucius groaned, but it was more in the line of an acceptance-of-the-situation sound rather than his usual rebellious sort.

"Come along to meet her. She's quite interesting, I daresay. You'll see."

CHAPTER TWENTY-ONE

Two Weeks Later

THE HOUSEHOLD HAD settled into a somewhat normal routine in the fourteen days since Miss Docia's and Lord Perlsea's additions to Stonemare. Additional wages would not be unwelcome. But how did one go about requesting such a thing without overstepping or being dismissed outright? She sucked in an indignant breath. When the devil did she become frightened of her own shadow? Frankly, Lord Pender and Mr. Oshea would be in a pickle if she left.

At least the weather was acting cooperatively—cold, rather than snowy or rainy—allowing her daily escape for bracing walks over the moors. Occasionally, she could even turn her face up to see a hazy sun breaking through the heavy clouds.

She encouraged her charges to take advantage as well. Fresh air was vital to a healthy constitution, she believed. It had a way of clearing the fog from one's mind no matter one's age.

Lord Pender had remained scarce since the day of Lord Perlsea's return from Eton. And opportunities of visiting with Mr. Oshea had been limited to quiet evenings in the library after the children were abed. Sadly, there hadn't been a repeat of that delicious kiss—

Verda groaned. She'd truly lost her mental faculties. He'd as much admitted to killing his own father. But when she looked at him, sat near enough to take in the heady scent he emanated, it drowned out any possibility he could do such harm to anyone, let alone his own father. Her conflicting emotions were the only dissonance in an otherwise unexpected harmony in her added duties.

Well, there was Miss Docia's objections to Julius's presence at the lessons. It was a conundrum in which Verda happened to agree. No matter how adorable she found Julius, he was a baby and a distraction. As a result, Maura was usually in attendance for the lessons as well. From the corner of her eye, Verda would catch her smiling about some comment one of the children had made.

These were the sorts of issues she preferred contemplating on her daily outings. She gazed out over the blustery winter day, lighted by the muted sun. The waves crashing below offered no solution that she could bring to Noah that would comfort him without alienating him.

When all was said and done, and in truth, what did it hurt for Julius to be in the library for their ongoing lessons? Surely, the discussions would embed in his developing brain, right? Noah deserved her constancy. He was her champion as much as she was his.

She let out a frosted breath and took the path back to Stonemare. To her surprise, Miss Docia and her maid were dashing across the lawn. Hmm. An intriguing sight, though Verda hadn't detected any further animosity from Docia regarding the girl's initial accusations. And it did thrill Verda to realize how her words for fresh air had been taken to heart.

Surprisingly, there was something infinitely satisfying and humbling in working with children. To know one was taking a hand in molding the future.

Verda entered the hall and handed off her cloak, bonnet, and gloves to Fletcher.

Mr. Winfield appeared as mysteriously as Baldric, startling her. "One moment, Miss Fairclough."

"Yes, Mr. Winfield?"

He held out a brown wrapped package. "This arrived for you."

"Oh, thank you."

The butler stepped away.

It was from Papa. She stripped off the paper and grinned before unfolding the missive.

Dearest Daughter,

I cannot fathom your reasons for wanting this ridiculous book of essays, by a woman, no less. But here it is. I trust all else is well. I'm vastly perturbed that you abandoned all my plans for you and Rathbourne, who has since given me the direct cut.

While I was greatly encouraged by your note, you might have been more forthcoming about your presence in Lord Pender's home. I thought you and the earl were to marry and I was disappointed to learn you are there as merely a governess.

Perhaps you could put a bug in Oshea's ear regarding his henchman? The man is a brute. Better yet, speak with Lord Pender. There is still time to work your wiles on the earl. T'would benefit both you and I. Why, I am hardly allowed my leave. I lay all this at your feet, Verda, for the ungrateful daughter you are.

I expect to hear news regarding favorable nuptials soon.

Yrs,
Krupt.

Not *Father*, not *Papa*. Krupt. Ungrateful. That was what her father believed of her. Rarely had he offered a kind word for her since Mama's death. Nothing of the years she'd spent handling the housekeeping duties, his matters of business. The list was endless, and for what? To be chastised because she couldn't stand the thought of that horrid duke laying his hands on her, let alone tying herself to him for all of eternity?

Guilt-bidden tears blinded her. She blinked them back and looked at the note again. What did he mean by Mr. Oshea's henchman being a brute? And of that nonsense of his not being allowed to leave? She certainly didn't wish to see him hurt. He was her father. She stuffed the missive in a pocket. Mr. Oshea had a few questions to answer.

Docia flew in from a back hallway, breathless and wind-blown.

"Miss Fairclough?" Noah stood in the arch of the library. "We should start before my Julius wakes."

"By all means," Docia sneered. "Our schedules must revolve around an infant."

The conundrum was rearing his head. "That's enough, Miss Docia."

"It's *Lady* Docia," she bit out.

"Actually, it's Miss Docia, Miss Docia. Once you are present-ed, you will be Miss Hale."

She pulled up and spun about, fury vibrating her small body. "I beg your pardon?"

"You are a viscount's daughter. Not an earl's, nor a mar-quess's, nor a duke's. The proper address for a viscount's daughter is 'Miss.' If you like, I'm sure we can locate a copy of *Debrett's* that could help clear the matter."

Her mouth gaped. "But my mother—"

"Indulged you to your own detriment."

"But *you're* a 'miss.'"

Verda handed down her own version of a peerage smile. "I'm also a member of the beau monde, Miss Docia. My father is Baron Krupt."

It took all of two minutes for this reality to work its way into Docia's brain and to her mouth. "I still outrank you, Miss Fairclough."

"Not in the classroom, dear." Verda indicated the way to the library with an outstretched hand. "Shall we?"

Docia stomped past her in a huff.

Verda followed her inside, where Noah and Lord Perlsea awaited. Julius, too, without Maura, for their afternoon session.

Inside, it felt as if she'd swallowed a pile of rusted tacks, and they tore at the lining of her stomach. Hearing the baby's sweet coos were a balm she suddenly craved. When she thought how frightened she'd been when she'd first arrived at Stonemare. To fear such a tiny being was almost ludicrous in retrospect.

The basket, situated in its usual spot near the fire, beckoned her. She hurried over and leaning in, caressed the back of his tiny fist with her forefinger. "Good afternoon, Master Julius," she whispered. She closed her eyes and collected her wavering fortitude. A second later, the disordered faculties once more ordered, she drew in a deep breath. "Are you ready for today's lesson on history?" Collected wits, she spoke in her most stern governess guise. It was all a front, after all.

Groans sounded from behind. Verda straightened and faced her charges. She held up the book.

Only Noah reacted, his spine going rigid, excitement lighting his gray eyes. "Is that Mrs. Fulhame's book on dyeing?"

The tightness in Verda's chest gave way, allowing her to grin back. "It is, indeed." She turned the book around and read, *"An Essay on Combustion With a View to a New Art of Dying and Painting, Wherein the Phlogistic and Antiphlogistic Hypotheses Are Proved Erroneous."*

"I don't wish to learn about dying." Docia sniffed.

Lord Perlsea, unengaged as ever, drummed his fingers on the table.

"It's not about being dead." Noah's small chest puffed out. "Mrs. Fulhame was a chemist, wasn't she, Miss Fairclough?"

Lord Perlsea's fingers stopped while skepticism covered Docia's expression.

"Master Noah is quite correct. Mrs. Fulhame was a chemist who studied a process of infusing fabrics with precious metals."

"Like what?" Lord Perlsea asked with a narrowed gaze that mimicked his uncle's.

"Gold and bronze and silver," Noah said.

"A woman scientist?" Miss Docia scowled. "You said we were to study history, not fairy tales."

Verda caught Docia's eyes and held them. "Are you not the least bit curious on how a *woman* made such headway in a man's world?"

The silence in the room was poignant then broken by Lord Perlsea. "I am."

Docia's gaze shot to him and back. "Me too," she said quickly.

Somehow, Verda managed to restrain sending her eyes skyward. "Excellent." She took a seat at the table and opened Elizabeth Fulhame's book of essays. "'*As Hydrogen, or the base of inflammable air, seems to act an important part in the experiments, and is, according to some chymists, pure phlogiston itself; I have therefore assigned the first chapter…*'"

Verda was halfway through Mrs. Fulhame's first experiment of gold using sulfuric acid before Julius's cries startled everyone at the table.

"Why is that infant allowed out of the nursery?" Docia demanded. Her churlishness upset the equilibrium of the session to an outrageous degree.

Mainly Noah's.

He was instantly on his feet, his hands squeezed into fists, his face a twisted snarl. "It's too cold for him up there. Besides, Miss Bash needs her rest. My Julius woke three times last night."

"And why must you refer to him by that foolish name?" Apparently, Docia did not have the wherewithal to quit, as shown in her step closer to Noah. While Verda hadn't witnessed further mistreatment of Olive, the girl had since redirected her animosity to Julius, thus setting Noah on the edge of a thin cliff.

His dislike of Docia bordered on true hatred and it worried Verda. Such depths of his loathing affected not just his attention on his studies, but spilled over, disrupting everyone's ability to participate. Not to mention Julius's sensitivity to Noah's mood changes.

"Why don't we take a short break? I believe it may be time for Master Julius to eat," Verda said. "I think we could all use a small refreshment." She stood from the table then went to the pull chord. Mrs. Knagg would soon have everyone fed and calmed down.

But Docia stomped from the chamber as only an indignant, eleven-year-old miss could—or so Verda imagined. She never remembered behaving that way herself.

Noah went to the basket and lifted Julius out.

"Do you have his cylinder, Master Noah?" Verda asked him.

"Of course, ma'am."

As Noah settled in the large chair with the baby, Verda found the glass bottle and handed it to him.

Lord Perlsea rose from the table and wandered over. "Do you need help?" he asked his brother.

Verda stilled for this unexpected—what seemed to her—olive branch.

Noah, concentrating on situating Julius, didn't look up. "No."

"I'll sit here with you just in case," Lord Perlsea said.

The familiar stubbornness mottled Noah's expression, jarring Verda into stepping in before the next wave of contention could take hold. "I believe what Lord Perlsea is trying to convey, Master Noah, is his interest in meeting his new brother."

Noah met her pointed look. "Oh. Lucius, this is my Julius. Papa gave him to me to take care of." His nose wrinkled, adorably so. "Kind of like a puppy."

Lord Perlsea leaned in for a closer look. "He sure is tiny."

"Yes. He really likes me. I think he'll really like you too because we're his brothers. He won't care what that stupid Docia says. She's a girl."

Verda took umbrage at that. In her view, one must defend one's gender where one could. "I'm a woman as well, Master Noah."

"That's true, Miss Fairclough." He glanced at his older brother. "My Julius does like Miss Fairclough, even though she was afraid of him at first." After a second, he added, "He likes Miss Bash too."

"I'm in good company, it appears," Verda murmured. "But in all fairness, we must do our utmost to include Miss Docia. It is the right thing to do."

Lord Perlsea glanced at her, and for the first time since he'd been at Stonemare, she detected a touch of softening, laced with amusement from him. It lifted a great weight from her shoulders.

Two down, one to liberate, she thought, heading for the door. Perhaps Docia was the one most in need.

CHAPTER TWENTY-TWO

LATER THAT EVENING, Sander handed Miss Fairclough a glass of brandy and lowered beside her on the settee rather than his usual place in the wingback chair. The winds had picked up in the afternoon that had branches tapping the windows. An ideal backdrop for Bach's Toccata and Fugue in D Minor.

The fire blazing the hearth reflected the brilliant highlights in Miss Fairclough's hair and matched the blood racing Sander's veins. He searched his lust-filled brain for something to deflect the urge to take her in his arms. "I understand you received a package today?"

Her emerald eyes flashed. "I did, indeed. Papa sent Mrs. Fulhame's book of essays." Her calm tone seemed forced.

"And how is your doting papa?"

"Perhaps you should tell me?" she returned.

Sander frowned, confusion rippling through him.

She pulled a piece of vellum from her pocket and slapped it into his hand.

Setting his tumbler aside, Sander stood and moved closer to the candelabra. He unfolded the scrap and quickly glanced through it. A pike impaled his chest coated with fear and anger. He grasped the anger, snapping the missive in the air and glared at her. "He wishes you to marry my brother?" The absolute gall of the man had Sander irate enough to jump on his horse, bound for London, to beat the baron to a bloody pulp.

"You are missing the entire point, sir." She jumped to her feet and waved out her hand, her annoyance grating over him. "You know very well, *doting* is the last thing my self-absorbed father is."

Sander hissed in a breath through his teeth and let it out more slowly. "Was accepting the position as governess just an excuse for access to my brother?"

"Oh, for the sake of heaven." She returned his glare, her vexation evident. "You big lummox. When you engaged my services, I was under the impression Lady Pender was still amongst us." Her emerald eyes glittering with fury, she snatched the letter from him and stuffed it back in her pocket. "I cannot believe this—"

But he'd heard enough of his own dimwittedness. Without a thought for protocol, civility, *decency*, he had her by the upper arms and his mouth was crashing over hers. Waves of unfulfilled need tore through him, spiking his blood like an overindulgent drunkard.

Her shock gave him access to the warm, velvety confines of her mouth, her tongue scraped against his, and her arms crept about his neck. Pert breasts heaved against his chest and sent blood-hot surges of sensation straight south. A result with a disastrous outcome if he couldn't manage to break away.

She moaned.

And he couldn't. His arms went around her and tightened.

She seemed as hungry as he. She devoured as much as she was devoured.

His punishing kiss was returned tenfold. He jerked his mouth from hers and with fumbling fingers, attacked the buttons at her neck and parted the offending wool. He traced the fire-glowing skin he'd exposed with his tongue. It tingled with the alluring spice that was all her.

"Oh, my," she whispered. Her hand slid from his neck to his shoulders and planted on his chest. "Stop, sir. Please."

Each word was a dagger in his sternum, the third one finally piercing his lung. He would swear the oxygen hissed out of that sliced wound and a piece of his heart with it. "Forgive me, Miss

Fairclough. Verda…" he finished on a whisper.

"You have an effective way of dissolving a disagreement, sir." The husky tremor of her voice teased a smile from him. She was much less composed than she let on. She cleared her throat. "What of this brutish henchman Papa speaks of?"

"Bah! Gnash Denholm is as gentle as a child's stuffed bear. Admittedly, he comes across more large and terrifying."

"H-He's not brutal, then?" Her small voice was a grip about his throat.

He guided her to the settee and lowered, pulling her down beside him. He grasped her hands. "Only if you count following the baron about town and bodily removing him from the tables he sits in on at the variety of hells he's prone to visit."

"That's it?"

"Miss Fairclough, the only thing your father suffers from is acute embarrassment." He leaned his forehead against hers, drawing in the soft, powdery fragrance of violets so out of place for the dead of winter. To his utter astonishment and relief, she did not pull away.

"Oh. That's all right, then." Again, the husky timbre breathed fire on the low-burning embers he'd barely banked.

He couldn't have torn himself away for all the king's jewels. He closed his eyes and touched her nose with his. A feathered caress that ignited the kindling that his skin resembled. The effect was instantaneous. He tilted his head. Let his breath mingle with hers. One of brandy and mint.

The tip of her tongue touched her bottom lip, but his mouth was so close, it brushed his as well, and he captured it, sucking it into his own mouth. The cock in his breeches joined the admiralty in its salute to her all-encompassing beauty. It had no care that she wore a dull, brown, woolen frock with its una-dorned neck that covered, what he envisioned, enchanting breasts.

He molded his lips to hers, exploring her mouth with sensa-tions exploding on his tongue. Heat infused his skin and he pulled back and yanked at the fastenings of his waistcoat. He glanced up, catching those sensuous green eyes, reflecting the fire. "Verda?" he whispered.

She licked her lips again, sending another surge of lust plowing through him. "It's just like I'd dreamed… Sander."

Waistcoat forgotten, and with a harsh moan, he took her mouth once more. And not so gently. He wanted to crawl inside her, let her push his haunting past from his mind. *The past.* He jerked back, his breaths rapid, his heart pounding painfully against his ribs.

Concern filled her eyes. Not disgust. Not anger. Not mirth. She grasped his hands. Hard. Their strength sunk into the depths of him. "What is it, Sander? Tell me."

His eyes snapped to hers, but he quickly pulled away. Turned from her. Shoved his hand warmed by hers through his hair. "I'm not who I seem." His voice sounded so raspy, he hardly recognized it as his own.

Her arm slipped around his shoulders, her head rested on his upper arm. "Because you believe you killed your father," she said. Her matter-of-factness startled him.

Slowly, his gaze met hers. Dark, luminous pools he would give his life to fall in and drown. "How did you know?"

"I heard you talking to the earl."

His eyes squeezed shut. Pain manacled his chest.

"Please—" Her beg etched through a crack.

"I had to save him. Father hated him." He glared at her, implored her to understand. "There was no one else."

"In case you haven't noticed," she said with a small bitter smile. "I'm not offended. I'm not even shocked."

He stilled. She was right. He speared her with a sharp look. "Why not? Why are you not offended or shocked?"

Her arm fell away, leaving him with a cold that burrowed deep despite the blaze across from them. She stared into the fire and he thought she didn't see the fire at all. After a moment, she shook her head then turned and faced him. "You did what you had to do. That's heroic," she said firmly. "Not villainous. Besides, I think there is more to the tale."

He took her face in his hands—how could he not?—stared into her eyes. "I'm no one's hero."

"I beg to differ." Her breath caressed his lips. "You're your brother's hero. Whether he says it aloud matters not. You're Miss Docia's hero. I saw how you hugged her, and she's tough."

In that moment, something changed in Sander. The restriction stealing his breath loosened.

Her eyes fell to his mouth and she licked her lips.

"And you? Am I your hero?"

"I have no need of a hero," she said primly, clearly teasing him.

"Oh, how desperately I want you," he growled. *Desperately want to marry you.*

"I want you too." Her fingers crept to his with a touch as light as air.

He brought her hand to his mouth. Silky, smooth, and scented like spring. Her other arm circled his neck.

Breathless with anticipation, he waited to see what she desired from him. That wait was interminable. Forever. Even as she leaned forward and feathered his lips with hers. But when the tip of her tongue dampened his lips, he opened his mouth and let her in.

Control was underrated, but he clung to it as if it were his last grip with sanity. She deserved his name, not just his bed. Her hand remained in his, and the restraint in not pressing it to the front-fall of his breeches would likely destroy him.

He pulled away slightly. Her lips were swollen. Moaning, he worked his lips to just below her ear. The violets brought to mind a springtime day in a meadow full of the purple petals and the clash of her flaming hair amid the clusters. He licked the erratic pulse in her neck.

"Might I touch you?" he whispered.

"Only if I am allowed the same privilege," she whispered

back.

His fingers worked more of the buttons down the front of her gown. "Oh, yes." He peeled the wool from her shoulders and set his lips on the soft, creamy skin he found there. The sensation released some of the intensity in his tightly coiled muscles. He tugged at the ties of her chemise and drew it down to reveal a swell of her breast.

Her breath hitched, stilling him.

Her hands flattened on his chest.

The muscles there twitched.

She tugged at his cravat, then parted his shirt. She leaned in and kissed him at the opening, singeing his skin. "You smell of… the crashing sea, the blowing winds, the… bracing air. All that I crave—"

The long clock in the entryway bonged and she jumped.

Her spine jerked ramrod straight. "Oh, no," she whispered. Her horrified expression was a direct jab from Gentleman Jackson himself. "You must think me the worst sort of harlot—"

"Never." He adjusted and tied her chemise back in place. "Please. Don't. Not a word. This is my fault."

She shoved his hands away, glaring at him. "Is it? Do you believe me fickle of mind? Destined for Bedlam?" She poked him in the chest, one curved nail jabbing him. "I must return to my chamber, sir. In the event Master Noah needs my assistance with Master Julius."

Sander was dumbfounded. Speechless. Mortified that she doubted his desire.

"After the debacle with Mrs. Lyall, I feel it imperative he can find me if there is a need." She stood and wobbled as if her knees were about to give out.

He stood too and finished tucking her securely into her drab, woolen frock. "I fear the only one destined for Bedlam, Miss Fairclough, is me." He completed his task and grasped her upper arms. "You are much too good for me, but I find the idea of not having you too horrific to contemplate. Come, I shall walk you to your chamber."

Tension eased from her shoulders and she smiled. "Thank you. It is a long walk and quite frightening at times. One never knows when a ghoul will appear from the shadows."

"I am not a ghoul."

"Specter, then."

"No."

"Apparition."

"In your dreams, Miss Fairclough." He grabbed the candelabra and met her at the door.

"That is my greatest fear," she said softly.

Sander paused, facing her, frowning at the tone. "What?"

"That you are an apparition in my dreams." Her dramatic sweep from the library and up the stairs had him hurrying in her wake.

COLD AIR OUTSIDE the library went far in cooling the heat searing Verda's body. The urge to stop and press her legs together to keep an unseemly moisture from seeping onto her thighs nearly felled her. Only the fact that Mr. Oshea followed so closely saved her from such humiliation. Her nipples were hard beneath her dress and the thin silk of her chemise did not deter the desire of wishing it was his fingers or—she swallowed hard—his mouth to ease the traitorous wantonness she couldn't seem to stem. *How mortifying,* she chastised herself. Yet it was difficult to muster any guilt.

Blast it, she was nine and twenty. Firmly on the shelf and quite proud of the feat. Marrying the Earl of Pender was as desirable as latching on to the Duke of Rathbourne. A thought that sent chills over her skin, and not in a pleasing way.

The long walk to her chamber was companionable, considering she'd lost her head and wanted to strip Mr. Oshea to his small clothes. She'd been rendered half-naked herself in the library. She shivered with the lust that had kidnapped her senses. She just needed to keep the sentiment to the forefront of her mind—it was just *lust*.

They reached her chamber and Mr. Oshea pushed through the door without so much as a by-your-leave.

"What are you doing?" she hissed. "You'll wake my maid."

"That's ridiculous," he shot back. "I'm just going to stir the fire—" His eyes went to the bed and he pulled up. His thumb flew out, pointed in that very direction. "Who the devil is in your—"

Slowly, the lump rose to sitting. Lizzie rubbed her eyes. "Oh, miss, you're back." She blinked and pulled the covers to her chest. "Er, sir…"

"What is your maid doing in your bed?"

Before Verda could stop Lizzie, she blurted out, "The lizards, sir."

Mr. Oshea lifted a brow at Verda. "Lizards?"

"A whole family of them," Lizzie went on. "The mistress has nightmares, you see."

"That's enough, Lizzie. Mr. Oshea has no interest in my dreams."

His mouth quirked at one end. A mouth that had tasted as delicious as it now looked. A mouth she envisioned as most skilled. In ways she couldn't begin to imagine but oh-so-wished to experience. "Ah, but I have every interest in your dreams, my dear." The low deep intonation raised the hair at her nape.

Exactly what she feared.

"Noah's welcome to Stonemare gift, I take it?"

Verda's lips compressed.

"I'll speak with the lad on the morrow."

A step forward put her nose nearly to his chest. She lifted her finger, almost touching his. "You'll do no such thing." She glanced at the bed, but Lizzie had snuck away, the little coward. "I can handle my own conflicts, thank you very much." She dropped her hand and moved to the fire, took up the poker herself, and prodded the embers before tossing on another log. "Besides, Noah has since apologized."

Silence filled the space and she glanced at him over her shoulder.

Her words seemed to take him aback. Inside, she melted like hot butter in an iron pot. "Oh, my." She went and stood before him. "You are unused to anyone looking out for themselves, aren't you?"

His eyes closed, then opened. The swirling gray was no match for the storms beyond the windows.

"I think we are alike in this," she said so softly, he likely didn't hear. She took his hand, brought it to her lips, then laid her cheek against its back side. "I don't need saving, Sander"—funny how quickly she'd adjusted to his given name—"but I thank you. No one's ever wished to save me before. It's a nice feeling." She lowered his hand and let go. "Quite nice, indeed."

CHAPTER TWENTY-THREE

ERPLEXED. SANDER STAGGERED to his chamber, *perplexed,* by Verda's claim of independence. Who was he if he couldn't save a person he cared for?

He'd thought a cold bath would cool his ardor, but… no. All it had taken was the warmth of plum-plump lips against his hand then the softness of her cheek against the roughness of his skin to shift his fervor of taking her before the fire to pulling her against his chest and keeping her there for all of eternity.

Had she meant it? *Yes.* She guarded her independence with the same fierceness Noah protected his infant brother.

But the contents of her father's missive lodged in his chest. What if she decided Damien was no longer a threat? He was an earl to boot and certainly trumped a mere mister. The thought sickened him as he reached his chamber. He stirred the fire to dispel the chill from the air and dropped on the nearest seat, leaning his elbows on his knees. A sense of despondency banded his lungs. He rested his chin on the back of his right hand to stare into the slow-catching fire. It tingled with the warmth of her cheek that he was certain had seared his skin for life.

His gut tightened with a fear so great, he jumped up and paced his chamber, searching for an answer that couldn't be found. Not there at any rate. Jesus. The uncertainty was enough to eat a man alive.

"Uncle Sander?"

Sander started. His gaze flew to the door where Lucius stood in the opening, barefoot and nightshirt hanging to his calves. "Damn it, Lucius, what the devil are you doing up at this hour? Come by the fire. You'll freeze your arse off. This blasted monolith is nothing but an ice tomb."

Lucius strolled to the fire and held his hands toward the heat. "Papa's returned," he said, turning around and facing Sander.

He frowned. "Oh? When was that?"

"A few hours ago." Disgust covered his features. "He was drunk, as usual. I asked him if he brought me a child to take care of too."

"Good God. I can't imagine his reaction…" His voice trailed off.

Lucius rubbed the side of his head. "He boxed my ears."

Another item he silently added to the list to blast his brother over. Sander nearly rubbed his hands together, actually relishing the confrontation.

"Do you think Father killed Mama?"

Shock clubbed him in the sternum. "What?"

Lucius picked at his nightshirt. "Maybe the question is, did grandfather kill our grandmother?" The words sucked the oxygen right out of the chamber.

"Where did you even hear such a thing?" Sander breathed out. He'd been the only one standing at his mother's door that night when Sander had been six, listening to his father's tirade from behind the door. Then the bone-crunching hit followed by his mother's sudden silence.

But he'd never mentioned it to another soul.

Lucius's expression again wrinkled in his disgust. "Father's rambling discourse. I could hardly make sense of him. Was he speaking of Grandfather killing Grandmother? I thought Julius offed Mama."

"Good God, Lucius. Your father did not kill your mother. She did die in childbirth. It's a common enough cause for women." Sander stared at his thirteen-year-old nephew. Lucius may not have liked or appreciated Eton, but certainly some of its polish was taking hold. "Perhaps I require a word with your father."

"He's asleep in his study with his head on his desk," Lucius said. "I thought you might want to know."

"Thank you. I'll take a look." Sander rose and went to the door. "Did you wish to wait here for me to return? You're welcome to do so, of course."

"No." Lucius followed him to the door. "I know Noah is taking care of Julius, but I think I should remain nearby… just in case he needs help."

"You're very wise, Lucius." A smile tugged at him. "I suspect thinking like that is what will carry you through your education."

Sander watched as Lucius made his way to the stairs for the third level and disappeared. No man could have better nephews than he. He wished Damien could see the same value in his sons. Shaking his head, Sander took the main staircase to the ground floor and found Damien right where Lucius said he'd be.

Damien's head lay on the desk, on folded arms, his face turned toward the windows. The black coverings had been ripped down and lay in heaps along the floorboards. The room was chilly and Sander tossed more fuel on the fire. He poured himself a brandy and went to the windows. The gloom seeped through to his bones. Northumberland was not for the faint-hearted. He sipped at his brandy and waited.

The wait wasn't long.

The chair creaked and Sander peered over his shoulder. "He lives."

"What the devil are you doing, standing in the dark?" Damien's raspiness scraped over his skin.

"Quit hitting your sons upside their heads or I shall take the same method of punishment to you."

"You've a lot of nerve dictating to me," he growled.

"Regardless, I'll trounce you if I catch you at it."

"He was insolent."

"And you weren't coherent enough for an intelligent conversation."

"There's that," Damien acknowledged grudgingly. "Why's he going to you?"

"Because, and I quote, 'in your rambling discourse,' you mentioned our father killed our mother."

Damien leaned back, pressing his fingers into his forehead. "I believe I could use another drink."

"You'll have to serve yourself. Intelligent conversation and all."

He sighed. "Did I really say that?"

"I don't know where else he would have come up with such a question."

"No, I don't suppose he would."

Sander moved to one of the desk-facing chairs and sat down. "I hadn't realized you knew the truth."

"I overheard Mama's companion speaking with the midwife that night," he said. The shadows in his eyes told of other specters haunting him. "So, you knew the truth, then?"

"I… Yes. I wanted desperately to see her. Father shoved me out of the way and slammed the door in my face. I heard him hit her. She didn't even cry."

"Dear God." Damien rose from his chair, his gait unsteady, and went to the brandy decanter. He poured out a couple of fingers and knocked it back. "You weren't but six."

A twinge of humor touched Sander. "To your shocking age of seven." Then, serious. "Yes. I was only six. And terrified."

Damien's demeanor firmed. "I don't want them mentioning Father."

"Might it not be wiser to share that particular sentiment with the boys? Children have brains. Women, also, as I was recently, and firmly, informed."

The imposing earl shifted into a pious being Sander didn't recognize. "One doesn't share that sort of information with *children*. Are you bound for Bedlam?"

"I happen to believe the truth is better no matter how ugly. Fewer secrets to loom out of the past at the most inconvenient times."

But Damien was having nothing of it. "You'll not breathe a word, damn you. I'll kill you myself."

Sander stood and set his glass next to the decanter. "Of course, if that is your desire, but secrets never bode well. Good night, Damien."

CHAPTER TWENTY-FOUR

VERDA ACCEPTED HER cloak and gloves from Fletcher as Mr. Winfield, who was Mrs. Knagg's polar opposite in every possible way, stood by watching. "Thank you, Fletcher. I shan't be long. Mr. Winfield."

"Miss Fairclough. Miss Fairclough."

Verda clasped her cloak at the throat and turned.

Miss Docia tripped down the stairs, her steps dainty, infinitely feminine. Her windblown, golden locks, not at all in the first state-of-fashion, much-too-old-for-her, as was her norm. "Are you for your morning stroll, miss? Might I join you?"

With a quick smile, Verda indicated Docia's hair. "Have you not been out already?"

Her hand flew to the loosed strands, red staining her cheeks, eyes flashing, mouth frowning. "That blasted Olive. I vow when Papa returns I'll have him turning her out so quickly—well, she can forget any recommendation from *me*," she snapped. As if recalling who she stood near, Miss Docia glanced up, guilt-ridden eyes wide. "Er, forgive me, miss. She just makes me so angry."

Verda inclined her head, biting the inside of her cheek. "Forgiven, my dear. Recognizing our actions is the first step in correcting them. Of course, you may accompany me."

"Thank you, miss. My cloak, Fletcher," she said with a sharpened edge.

Once more, Verda was forced to restrain an eyeroll to the heavens, instead waiting with undue patience for Fletcher to assist the impertinent chit with her cloak and for said chit to feel Verda's eyes upon her.

It took only seconds for Docia's body to still, then for her to slowly raise her eyes to Verda's.

She was a bright child.

The girl blinked and, without a tear to be seen, shifted her focus to Fletcher. "Thank you for your assistance, Fletcher. Please forgive my brusqueness." Her delivery was so sweet, Verda had to remember to clamp her mouth shut.

Verda smiled at the footman. "We'll return soon," she told him because she couldn't envision more than twenty minutes alone with the girl without even Julius as a distraction. Verda took herself to task and vowed to make up for her insolence toward a young girl who was essentially alone, but for a sixteen-year-old maid for company.

With a shake of her head, Verda stepped under the portico. It was eye-opening as always with the cold air stealing her breath. The view never failed in reminding her she was alive and not trapped in a chamber with no food, water, or fire. They took the path to the forest with the wind whipping their cloaks.

"You walk this way every day?" Docia's head was down, minding her steps. Or perhaps watching for twigs that might scratch the nice kid leather of her half-boots.

"Most days. The rain makes a walk difficult and snow virtually impossible. But I embrace the freedom it allots me."

"It's cold."

Verda grinned. "Yes. But I love it."

A delicate shiver went over the girl just as they reached the edge of the forest and the forked path. She stopped and peered at Verda. "Which way?"

The path to the left led along the cliffs and to the right, the open moors.

The ocean was irresistible, calming even, and Verda veered left, with the little princess following. They made their way over roots marring the path Verda had since learned to avoid.

"I was quite cross with you, you know," her companion said.

"Oh?"

"My mother always called me 'Lady Docia,'" she said softly. "I expect she believed I would marry a great lord someday. Eleanor did as well. I-I miss her, them." The wispy tonality tugged at Verda.

She stopped and turned to the girl. "I owe you an apology, Miss Docia. I am not known for a tempestuous personality, as I consider myself most pragmatic. Something of late has apparently upset that balance."

"Thank you, Miss Fairclough. I accept your apology."

Verda grinned. "Excellent, my dear." She turned and marched down the path. "Come now, the day is getting away from us."

The cliffs were especially gusty, but oh, how she loved the sound of the waves crashing against the rocks. There was something about the sight too. Its power, perhaps. No mere soul could escape such force on their own. Such ferocity had a way of reminding one of where one stood when it came to nature's laws—

The air left Verda's body in a harsh exhale and her body surged forward, breaking over the brink of the cliff.

"No!" The ear-piercing scream reached through.

A vortex of black spiraled through Verda in disorienting chaos. Seconds elapsed before she realized she was not flailing midair, but she lay flat on her stomach, her knees stinging with the force of the ground she'd skidded over. It took another moment to find the courage to open her eyes. She quickly closed them, her heart nearly leaping from her body. She couldn't stay there, not with her head hanging over the edge, witnessing the death she'd just defied. The shock of that fact was sudden as common sense reared, piercing the thickness of her skull.

"Oh, Miss Fairclough. Dear heavens. Please, please don't be dead. I'm sorry. I-I tripped." Docia's voice shook with panic. "Miss Fairclough?"

"I'm still alive, Lady Docia." Her voice cracked and she rolled to her back, breathing a prayer of thanks for the hard ground now supporting her head. She opened her eyes and hauled in the heavy, damp air. It was nice to appreciate the low, dark clouds from this angle rather than from the rocks below. A low moan emitted from her. She mustn't have suffered too greatly, as her humor remained intact. Either that or she was already dead and had entered purgatory and was awaiting the Almighty's judgment.

No. Docia kneeled beside her, stark terror filling her eyes. It appeared genuine—she hadn't time to manufacture tears.

The ground beneath Verda's head vibrated with heavy running steps.

She blinked and Sander appeared over her like an avenging angel. He lowered to one knee and slid a powerful arm beneath her neck then lifted her as gently as a newborn kitten. "What the devil happened?"

"I-I tripped," Docia stuttered. "I-I p-put my arms out t-to keep from f-falling and fell into M-Miss Fairclough." The tears fell then, her sobs lost in the waves below. "Your d-dress is t-torn. I-I shall m-mend it."

Grimacing, Verda was maneuvered to sitting where, indeed, there was a rip at the knees in her brown skirts. "I shall hold you to it," she promised the girl. And she would.

Sander's hands moved down one leg then the other, indecently so. "Nothing appears broken. Can you stand?"

"I-I think so." Her breathlessness was irritating. She *never* needed rescuing. Yet here she was.

He helped her to her feet, but she was more shaken than she'd first believed. Her knees wobbled so violently, it took a full moment to make herself release his arm. "Take it slow," he told her. His gaze moved to Docia. He yanked a handkerchief from a pocket and shoved it in her hand. "Where did you trip? Show me."

She wiped her tears away with still-shaking hands. She nodded and moved back down the path, stopped, then pointed.

"Here."

Sander followed her and went back down on one knee. He tapped his knuckles on a half-buried branch. "All right. Let's get back." He glanced at Verda. "Can you walk?"

She glared at him.

"Never mind," he said with a quick smile. "I can see the question is unappreciated."

The wind picked up, if that was even possible, but the trees shielded them from the worst of it.

"How did you happen upon us, sir?" Docia asked him.

That was an excellent question.

Docia's gaze lifted from the path to Sander and she tripped, but his quick reflexes saved her frock from the same fate Verda's had suffered. He balanced her and Docia stiffened. "Your hands— is that blood?"

Verda's eyes shot to his hands to what appeared streaks of dirt. How had she not noticed he hadn't worn gloves?

"One of the goats was hurt," he said. "I saw the two of you departing the castle and followed."

Docia's brows furrowed. "Is the goat all right?"

"He is, indeed."

"Another blasted boy," she groused.

"Miss Docia," Verda warned.

"Apologies, miss. I just feel overrun by them."

Verda knew the feeling. She couldn't seem to pull her gaze from the rusty streaks. "What happened to the goat?"

"The goat? Entangled with one of the horses."

Docia stopped and Verda nearly ran her down, giving truth to Docia's hands on her own back. She issued a silent apology. "What's that?" Docia was pointing into the shadows of the trees off the path.

Verda squinted but couldn't really make out anything but a pile of leaves.

Sander moved off the path and Verda followed. A sense of foreboding sent an icy breath brushing her neck that had nothing to do with the weather. Even more frightening was Docia's small hand creeping into hers.

"Good God," Sander breathed. For the third time in less than ten minutes, he was kneeling. "It's Colbert. He's hit his head."

"Is he d-dead?" Docia's high, child-like pitch raised ripples over Verda's skin.

Sander touched Colbert's wrist, then his neck. "Yes, he's dead." He glanced over his shoulder to Verda.

Verda couldn't move. The bodily fluids expelled from a dead body were like no other. Suddenly, she was eight years old again, trapped in her mother's bedchamber, surrounded by the dark. *I can't breathe.* He was speaking, his mouth was moving, but she couldn't hear him for the roaring in her ears. Her gaze moved back to Mr. Colbert.

"Miss Fairclough?"

The tiny voice penetrated her mind, but Verda couldn't tear her eyes from the dark mesh of gray hair. The blank stare of his opened eyes.

Her head rattled and she blinked. Sander's hands on her upper arms burned through her cloak. "Verda!" His stern tone penetrated her immobilizing shock, bringing her to her senses. "Miss Fairclough, listen to me. I need you to find Baldric. He should be in the stables. Can you do that?"

"Yes," she whispered. "Yes." Raspy, cracked.

"Good girl. Hurry, now."

She nodded, and gripping Docia's hand, ran for the castle with her heart threatening to fly from her chest. She blocked out all thoughts but one: *Find Baldric.*

"Why would someone kill Cracked?" her charge asked on a breathless rush.

"I've no notion." Verda could barely choke out the words.

From the boundary of the forest, the castle emerged, its battlements hidden within the clouds. Verda didn't stop until they reached the castle. She bent over to catch her breath. "Run inside. Have Mr. Winfield locate Lord Pender." A dose of rationality pinched her. "And do *not* come back out. Wait for me in the library. It might be best to keep this from the boys," she added.

At Docia's nod, Verda dashed for the stables. Behemoth drops of rain hit her nose as she rounded the side of the castle and the apparition who was not an apparition caught her up with one wiry hand. She let out a sharp yelp.

"Whoa there, miz. Where's the fire?"

"Fire…" She shook her head. "It's Mr."—she bent again to catch her breath—"Colbert."

"Cracked? What about 'im?"

"H-He's—" She swallowed hard. "Mr. Oshea n-needs you. He's on a path in the forest. Mr. Colbert's… h-he's—"

"Spit it out," he growled.

Verda glanced at his free hand; it was covered in rust streaks. "He's dead," she whispered.

Baldric strolled away in that ambling way of his that was likely faster than it appeared.

She fell against the castle's rough exterior, her body a mass of chaotic reactions: horror, shock, fear, even empathy. She'd never thought to experience those emotions all at once again in her entire lifetime. The horror moved to shock rendering her legs unequipped to hold her upright. Then fear that swamped her. Was someone out to hurt the children—Julius, Noah, Lord Perlsea, Docia? Her? Sander? Nothing made the slightest inkling of sense.

Surely not, she rationalized. Her head fell forward. *Poor Mr. Colbert.* There was nothing more she could do for him.

She was wasting time. The children needed reassuring. With a deep breath, she pushed away from the wall and strode to the portico on steadier legs.

Mr. Winfield met her at the door. "The children are in the library," he said by way of greeting.

She stripped off her cloak and gloves and thrust them at him. "How is Lady Docia?"

"Vibrating."

"Vibrating?"

His head angled to one side. "Perhaps shaken?"

"Yes, shaken. Have Mrs. Knagg send in refreshments. You say all the children are there?"

He inclined his head. "Even Master Julius."

Another jagged breath left her.

SANDER ROLLED CRACKED Colbert to his back. He ran his palm over the old man's face and closed his now-soulless eyes. The trace of warmth from his body indicated the attack had not taken place all that long ago.

"What the hell's going on?"

Sander rose from the ground and faced his brother. "Colbert's dead."

Damien stepped closer and peered down at the body. "No great loss," he said without an ounce of inflection. The tick in his lower cheek didn't escape Sander's notice, however, and Sander let the remark go. His brother wasn't as immune as he pretended.

Something Sander found reassuring. He hadn't been the only one Father's death had affected.

Seconds later, Baldric materialized like the ghosts he impersonated. "The woman was harried," he groused.

Sander's lips tightened.

Damien appeared not to have heard the stablemaster. "How did he die?"

Sander stepped over Colbert, the ground crunching beneath his boots. He bent down and picked up a bloodied rock, studied it then held it out.

The earl took it and ran his finger over a black, sticky substance. "Still wet."

"Old Cracked didn't deserve a crack on the head," Sander bit out.

"For the first time in years, my brother, I'm in complete agreement with you."

Well, that was a relief. Sander turned to Baldric. "We need to get the body out of here. I'll notify the magistrate."

"*I'm* the magistrate," his brother said.

"So you are. I hereby notify you that we have a dead body on Pender land." Fear mingled with biting sarcasm ripped through him. "In any event, the parish constable must be informed. How do you propose to the villagers that Cracked Colbert has met with a violent end and remind them they are safe from a similar fate?"

"That is the question." Damien shook his head. "I'm jesting. I don't know what to do."

Sander let out a harsh breath. "I'll ride to the village and speak with Broyle. He's the closest thing to a parish constable without traveling to Lesbury and he tends to have a decent head on his shoulder." He squinted in the shadows. "Baldric, let's get Colbert onto the cart and haul him to the village."

Chapter Twenty-Five

"*A DEAD BODY?*" Lord Perlsea jumped to his feet and ran to the windows, where it was impossible to see past two feet.

Verda attempted to rub the chill from her arms through her second-warmest frock. Her hands were clammy, her face hot, her mouth dry. Sitting was out of the question. The muscles in her legs were so tight that if she sat, she feared being able to rise again.

Docia was smoothing her hands over her muslin skirts. "Yes, I'm the one who spotted Cracked," she told her audience of two and a half—the half being Julius, who'd slept through her entire monologue.

Noah's mouth hung open, and Verda might have detected a tad of envy there as well. "Cracked Colbert, dead." He shook his head.

"I'm the future earl, I should have accompanied Uncle Sander and Baldric into the village," Lord Perlsea bit out.

"Oh, I don't believe that would have been wise, Lucius," Docia said. "You'd probably catch your death and that would leave Noah running things, and he's much too immature compared to you."

Docia's youthful affection for the young Lord Perlsea was clearly lost on Noah and, before Verda had time to step between them, Noah's finger was pointed in the young lady's face, not quite touching her nose. "You're nothing but a coddled brat."

Verda found her feet. "There will be no casting of aspersions, Master Noah."

"But she—"

"That's enough. We shall speak later. Miss Docia has a task to complete," Verda said. Docia groaned and had Verda been able to manage a grin, she would have been forced to hide it. She faced her charges' upturned faces from her position before the fire, her legs wobbling beneath her skirts. "We'll talk, then. Lord Perlsea, come away from the windows. Make certain you place the coverings back in place."

"These ugly, black curtains are abhorrent."

"That may well be, but they go far in keeping the room heated. Come by the fire." She invited the small group. "Now, shall we continue with Elizabeth Fulhame's experiments?" She was a little surprised that her voice held only the minutest tremor.

DUSK HAD SET in by the time Sander staggered into his chamber. A difficult feat, as his body was as responsive as an icicle on the Arctic Circle. The frigid rain hadn't ceased the entire day. He shivered then forced himself to disrobe.

All day, thoughts of Verda had haunted him. Her terror-stricken eyes in the depths of the trees, her stilled body, as if she'd grown roots like the trees surrounding them. Docia had shown less shock. Sander's instincts had been honed since the age of six when he'd stood outside his mother's chamber to have his father slamming the door in his face, never again to see his mother alive.

Those instincts now screamed at him. A shrill so intense, he was tempted to cover his ears.

And yet Verda had patted his arm, condescendingly so, telling him she didn't require saving. But if that was so, who would be there to save her from the ghosts so prevalent behind her dark-green eyes?

Fletcher entered his chamber hoisting the copper tub on his shoulders, followed by a couple of younger imps with pails of steaming water he'd requested.

Within an hour, Sander, now warmed through, refreshed and dressed modestly but comfortably, was equipped enough to face the uncertainties and contradictions that crafted the enigma that made up Miss Verda Fairclough. He suspected it wouldn't matter how long it took to know her. He would never learn enough to satisfy his curiosity.

Never.

The walk to her chamber was long and cold, but the anticipation of her flaming hair flowing over his fingers heated his blood. Whether or not she would allow such liberties mattered little. He spotted a stream of candlelight flickering beneath her door and rather than tapping at the bedchamber door where he suspected Lizzie was still residing, he approached the sitting room, as decorum dictated. He was only there to check on her, he assured himself.

He knocked lightly.

The door creaked back. "Mr. Oshea?"

The sight of that dark-red hair, drawn over one shoulder in a loose braid and clasped in her hand, sent his fantasies into a zealous riot that surged the fire in his veins to sweltering. He tamped back the urge to pull her into his arms. "I came to see how you were faring?" The words came out raspy.

"Well, thank you." Rubbing her upper arms contradicted her actual words. Body language spoke volumes. She was not well, *thank you.*

"May we speak?"

She glanced toward the door leading to the smaller bedchamber, not the master bedchamber of the suite. "Of course." She stepped back. The gray frock she wore did nothing for her fair complexion. She should be wrapped in silks, lace, and the finest muslins.

He stepped by her and was inundated by the powdery violet

he would never be able to banish from his senses. "Lizzie?"

She smiled. "You will be thrilled to know she has retaken residence in the smaller chamber. At her insistence, of course. Would you care for tea?"

"I would, indeed."

She took a seat on the settee, where a book lay face down. She swept it up, closed it, and set it aside. She poured out a cup.

"Two sugars," he said.

She stirred in the sugar, the delicate China tinkling, then held it out.

"What happened to you? In the forest," he added, as if she needed clarification.

The cup rattled and he quickly rescued it from her trembling fingers. "I-I don't know what you mean."

Without a single sip, he set the tea on the low table and shifted to beside her on the settee, took her hands in his. White and bloodless fingers told a different story than her mumbled words.

"Verda, what happened out there? I've never seen you…" He shook his head searching for the right word. "So… distressed."

She pulled her hands from his. "It was nothing."

"*Nothing*? Do not insult my intelligence, madam." With an inward wince at his sharpness, another thought struck him and he pinned her with a hard stare. "What was Lizzie inferring when she mentioned nightmares?"

Her emerald eyes glittered with self-contempt. She again reached for the pot of tea, but he brushed her away and refilled her cup himself. He tipped a dab of milk and started for the sugar.

"No sugar," she said, her voice not yet controlled, quaking.

He waited for her to say something. Anything.

Then… "Do you wish to enter a liaison?" Her question knocked the breath from him. And everything else in his puerile brain.

What of marriage—he wanted to rail. "In a heartbeat," he whispered, setting her cup beside his. He lifted his fingers, touching all that red fire dangling over her shoulder. Closing his eyes, he brought a handful to his nose and breathed in spring at the height of winter. Was there anything more delectable? He couldn't think of a single thing.

Her cold fingers lay over his. He flipped his hand and encased them, willing his warmth through her.

Sander leaned in, his head angled, and breathed in the gentle scent of her essence that mingled with the powdery violets. He rested one of her palms to his cheek. Its coolness was a soothing balm to his heated skin. He turned his lips to the softness of the inside of her wrist and, unable to resist, flicked out his tongue, smiled at her sharp gasp. His eyes opened and he glanced at the maid's sleeping chamber. "Are we safe from intrusion here?" he whispered.

"No," she returned.

"How shall we remedy that, Verda?" He was still smiling.

"I-I suppose we should remove ourselves… to my bedchamber."

"A very sound notion." He stood and pulled her to her feet. He swooped in for a quick, hard kiss, lest she thought to change her mind.

He needn't have worried. Her fingers clenched in his long-sleeved linen shirt. He pulled back. "Lead the way, my sweet."

To his relief, she didn't hesitate. He took no chances, however, keeping her hand hostage.

Only after entering her chamber did he release his hold to stir up the embers in the hearth and toss on more fuel.

His lady was not missish. She went around the chamber lighting candles before coming to his side and taking his hand. "You're so warm," she said. Her face was downturned to the link connecting them.

Sander brought her hand to his lips and brushed her knuckles. "Yes, and you'll be as well."

She shivered.

He let go of her hand and placed his on her shoulders and spun her about. He leaned in and dropped tiny kisses along the long length of her neck, testing its sensitivity with the tip of his tongue. "You will instruct me to stop at the first instance of uncertainty. Am I clear on this?" He nibbled between words, his fingers deftly at work on the fastenings, his proficiency because he'd visualized the task so often. Only every night since he'd met her.

"So masterful you are, Mr. Oshea." Her teasing, confident tone encouraged him.

The dress parted and he spun her to face him again. "Who is mastering whom, I wonder?" he whispered against those full, red lips. Her mouth parted and he tenderly accepted the invitation. His tongue caressed hers—better, her tongue explored his. His body coiled with a hunger that would not be satisfied with food, drink, even mild kisses. His cock was primed for her.

Only her.

He tugged her frock from her shoulders, pooling it at their feet. Her corset plumped her breasts, offering hardened nipples through the sheer chemise for his taking. He found the corset tie at her lower back and tugged it free, then loosened the boning.

All the while, her tongue chasing his, intensifying his craving until he was fit for the lunatic asylum. His erection pressed against her stomach, leaving no doubt of his desire. Her corset sagged and with a pained curse, he broke from her luscious mouth.

"What—"

"Shh. How am I to concentrate?" *Concentrate?* He was not jesting. His fingers trembled with the fastenings. But success was imminent and he dropped the offending garment to the floor. He freed the stays, sending them by way of her dress and corset, then brought his hands up filled with her chemise.

She lifted her arms for him to pull it over her head. He sent it flying and floating like a cloud. His hands landed on her back and drew her into him, her breast warm against his still too-clothed torso.

Her fingers crept behind his neck, her body pressing closer. It seemed she couldn't get close enough.

Not for him. Not until he could seed himself deep, feel the snug sheath of her inner fire.

Verda fumbled with the tie on his shirt. She tugged it from his breeches. He bent, giving her the same advantage he'd been granted. She sent her prize sailing and landing gracefully over a chair.

She started for his breeches, but he clasped her by the wrists and held her arms for a look at her. His gaze raked her body. Her breasts, the size of ripe peaches, beckoned—his mouth watered. The curling hair at her apex matched the hair on her head, all red fire. He smoothed his palms under her arms, his thumbs brushing her nipples and pebbling them to stiff nibs. The silkiness of her skin was irresistible as he made his way to her waist and flattened his hand on her stomach, inching his way through the dark curls and the dampness between her legs.

She let out a squeaked, "Oh."

He went on one knee and took the left breast in his mouth. A second later, he went for the right one. He burrowed his nose between them, brought his hands up on each side and cupped the perfectly shaped mounds, moaning.

Her knees wobbled and he came to his feet. They needed more stable ground for the play he envisioned.

He swept her from her feet and carried her to the bed. The spicy scent beneath the powdery violets overwhelmed him. He stood her before him and drew back the coverlets.

"Your breeches. You don't perform with them on…" Her brows furrowed. Adorably so. "Do you?"

"Not on your life," he growled, and he shucked them then swept her up and dropped her in the middle of his new leisure palace—a bed with the woman he couldn't imagine being in one without.

She landed with an "Oof."

He crawled up beside her and took her mouth with unfettered restraint. Her response was nothing short of Eden. Her mouth open, receptive, the giving and taking of unspoken promises. Her hands began their own exploration, searing a river of fire over his skin.

Exhilarating.

Enlightening.

Freeing.

If he didn't slow things down…

He didn't dare allow her near his cock. One feathered touch and it would be over. He flipped her to her back and laughed at another of her quick, surprised, "Oofs."

He pushed her knees apart. "Time to feast."

"*Feast?*"

"Will you be squealing like a mouse all night, my love?" He licked the inside of one thigh.

She gasped. "I fear so."

He inched closer to his treasure.

"Are you certain what you are doing is legal?"

"If not, we shall perish together." He dove in, for the spice that had been teasing him for what seemed years.

She squirmed beneath him and he grasped her hips to still her. She rocked against his mouth until she stiffened and flooded his senses with her release. He pressed his tongue against the living pulse of her then licked his way up her delectable body.

He rested his forearms on either side of her, kissed her. She didn't repel the taste of her on his lips. No. Not in the least. She returned his ardor with great enthusiasm. No hesitation.

Desperation rippled through him. He positioned himself at the core of her heat. His cock twitched. Her dampness drew him like a magnetic force. He pushed into her tight intimate channel. So snug. He pulled back and pushed again. Pull back, push in. "I'm sorry," he gasped, doing all he could to control the impulse to surge.

"No—"

He froze, unable to contain the pain-filled moan.

"Don't… stop," she panted. "*Please.*"

It was all he needed to hear—and he plunged forward.

Her legs wrapped his hips and he was gone, his mind a clean slate, his senses filled with scents of soft violets and tangy spice. His lips registered the satiny glide of her shoulder. He bit down lightly then licked. Her nails dug into his buttocks and he flew over the cliffs, pumping his seed into her, blinded by the bursts of white exploding behind his closed eyes.

"God," he whispered against her shoulder. He couldn't quite make himself shift to her side, but neither could he sag against her.

She drew her knees up alongside him and wriggled. His over-sensitized cock screamed. He moved one hand between them and pressed against the top of her sex. "Oh. Oh. Oh. Yessss." The squeal was back, but it sounded nothing like a mouse.

He maintained the pressure until the panting against his shoulder gave way to her cry and her body once more pulsed against the still-hard rod of his penis.

Seconds later, he forced himself to pull from her snug sheath and fell to her side, tugging her atop him, the silence in the chamber broken only by their shared, harsh breaths.

"I hurt you?" he asked.

"Never." Her soft whisper sated his heart with tenderness.

He rolled from the bed.

"You're leaving?"

"Never," he returned, smiling. Sander leaned in and dropped a kiss on her puckered lips before rising. The basin of water on the sideboard held fresh water, he was relieved to see, though cool. Something they could both use. He dipped a cloth and wrung it out. "This will help any soreness you experience."

"No, I don—"

He shot her a leering grin. "Spread your legs, darling. I'll be gentle."

She threw an arm over her eyes but did as he bid, gasping at the cold, as he could discern from the heat through the cloth.

He cleaned her up then rinsed the cloth, noting the smear of blood. The sight constricted his throat as he rinsed it as clean as he could get it then spread it out near the fire. He gathered their clothes in the event of a catastrophic moment then pinched out each candle's flame before crawling back in the bed. He took her in his arms, drawing his fingers through the red fire of her hair. "How do you feel?"

Her smile curved against his bare shoulder. "Debauched. Thoroughly and decadently debauched." She nuzzled her nose over his skin. "And quite sleepy."

"Then, sleep. I shall maintain a vigil for intruders."

"Lovely," she whispered. Seconds later, she relaxed beside him and her breathing leveled out.

Sander didn't wish to sleep. He wished to relive the magnetic forces and wondered briefly if his lustful partner had any knowledge of the illustrious Oersted and his studies on electro-magnetism. The thought rendered a grin. But it faded soon enough as the intruding thought of how he could manage to convince her to marry him. It felt as if he were walking a tightly woven rope constructed of thread.

He tugged her close, reveling in her body next to his and how right his world was in that moment. Perhaps he could guilt her into accepting his suit…

She would abhor that. Resent him for any kind of manipulation. Frustrated, he buried his nose in her hair and inhaled, deeply. The essence of her flowed through his veins and he fiddled with the silky strands of her hair.

The motion acted as a balm and with it, brought on the ability to let go, until drowsiness and the sense of contentment drifted over the chamber. Over him.

He could close his eyes… just for a moment.

CHAPTER TWENTY-SIX

"Open the door!" Verda screamed. She crawled atop the trunk Mama had demanded she shove in front of the door. "The door. Open it! Papa, please," she whimpered. The tears blinded her. She would never be warm again. The light. She needed light. But there were no candles. No fire. She climbed down and ran for the window. Yanked on the heavy drapes. She pushed a chair to the wall and climbed on that to reach the fastener. "I can't get it," she shrieked. "I can't get it." Her sobs hiccupped; her words broken. The latch was too hard for her fingers. They were too small… darkness closed in… she couldn't breathe—

"Verda. Darling, wake up."

Her body shook through the lethargy. She reached for the raspy depths of baritone.

"I'm here, love. That's it. Wake up."

Perspiration coated her skin. "Mr. Oshea?"

"How quickly you forget," he teased. "Must I remind you, it was Sander not so long ago. It's certainly acceptable for someone who's tasted—"

"Sander," she said quickly, her voice cracking but cutting him off before he could reveal any more humiliating revelations.

Laughter rumbled deep from his chest, vibrating against her naked body. He dropped a quick kiss on her lips. "You have nothing to be ashamed of, my love," he said, reading her mind.

Still, her face burned. Swallowing hard and unable to come up with anything coherent to say, she glanced to the windows. Black skies. The only light in the chamber exuded from the hearth in hot, red coals. Her pounding heart slowed to merely thumping. She breathed in through her nose and exhaled through her mouth. A technique that had always served in steadying her and did now.

"The nightmares…" His voice trailed.

She'd never be able to hold off his questions. Not now.

"Tell me."

If he'd demanded, perhaps she could have prolonged the inevitable, but it was his gentleness that stole beneath her defenses.

"My mother was ill, bedbound. Papa had spent us in dung territory, but of course I didn't know it then. I-I was eight."

He smoothed the hair off her forehead. His lips touched her. "Go on."

"Papa wasn't home. The housekeeper only visited twice per week. Even then, I began to realize Papa was a spendthrift and the financial situation was dire." She took a shallow and shaky breath. "Mama displayed paranoia tendencies. I couldn't possibly leave her alone," she whispered. "S-She had me move a trunk before the door." Verda stared up at the canopy she couldn't see in the dark. "It was quite heavy. I'm unsure how I even managed it." She turned her head toward him.

The fire revealed a silhouette of Sander on his side, elbow bent, cheek resting on his fist. His other hand brushed her shoulder, the side of her neck, her upper arm. Soothing motions, not sexual. Offered comfort, not lasciviousness.

"Eventually, Mama quit speaking. Her hands were cold." Her own hands squeezed into fists that rested between her breasts. She forced another breath. Deeper. "I tried to warm them, but nothing worked." The memories flooded her and spilled out. "I did everything I could think of. I piled all the clothes from her closet atop her. The fire had long since extinguished with no coal in the chamber. The candles had burned to nubs and drowned in their own wax."

"Dear God," he breathed.

"I-I couldn't get out. The trunk I'd moved"—the tears leaked from her eyes to her temples—"was too heavy. I can't understand that," she said with an unexpected wonder. "I mean, I'd moved it originally."

"Jolted."

Her gaze flew to him. "What?"

His hand tightened on her shoulder. "Your need to please your mother. Fear jolted a surge of energy and gave you strength."

"Oh." She took a minute to consider that, then nodded. "That makes perfect sense." She drew in another breath. "I remember being hungry but not thirsty."

"How long were you trapped?"

The word startled her. "Trapped? I-I was trapped. My mother was d-dead and I was… trapped… with her." She whispered the revelation, wondered again at how she'd survived such a horrid twist of fate.

"How long?" he said again. His voice was still soft, but there was an edge.

"I-I don't know. Three days, I think."

Tension shrouded their cocoon. "What happened then?" Again, that controlled countenance.

"The door rattled. I thought it was Papa. I was screaming for him to get me out. I-I couldn't stop screaming."

His fingers touched the side of her head. Seemed to soak up her tears. He leaned over her and kissed the offending moisture. "I swear if I see him, I'll see him paying his due."

She blinked and rested her cheek against his chest. "You mustn't blame Papa—"

"Who the devil *should* I blame, then?" he said through a stiffened jaw. "The eight-year-old girl trapped with her dead mother?"

"But—" The undercurrent of violence stopped her cold.

Sander was right. Papa had not only been irresponsible, he'd *left* her. Without the barest amenities for survival—no food, no coal—a small child who struggled to reach the latch on the window. Slowly, Verda rose to sitting. "Is that how you felt about… about your mother as well? That she was unable to protect you and your brother?"

His mouth opened—to refute her question?

She lifted her fingers and touched his lips. "You don't have to answer." His response mattered not, his presence assuaged her—the adult self of her and the child within who still harbored horrendous nightmares. He'd championed her, whether or not realizing so.

She faced him, making out the barest reflection of him in the darkness. Removing her hand, she leaned and leveled a kiss on him with every rioting emotion careening through her, felling him to his back. She moved atop his body, his warm hands spanning her waist. She used her tongue, just as he'd taught her.

The sensations were delicious and… medicinal. The feel of his tongue brushing hers, the warmth their bodies generated between them—she couldn't get close enough.

She swung one leg over, straddling him.

"Oh, you are adventurous." That low growl did something dangerous to her insides as he pulled her down to take one breast in his mouth.

Such sensuous torture.

The wetness between her legs that Sander had washed away returned with vengeance, warmed more by his body beneath hers. She pressed her sex against the hard length of his… "Is this magnificent specimen"—she wriggled on him—"referred to as a"—she angled her head, trying to remember what Mr. Colbert referred to as a, er,—"pikestaff?"

His mouth plopped from her breast with a harsh moan. "Where the devil did you hear—never mind. I don't wish to know. It's my cock." His hands tightened on her waist, halfway splaying her hips.

"This is an interesting position," she said, squirming about, her brows furrowing. "Is something like this possible?"

With a laugh that sounded just a tad maniacal, his hands adjusted her and he positioned his "cock" at her entrance. "Do what you will with me," he said in that gravelly sonance that raised the fine hairs on her skin, igniting a rush of fierce desire.

Her body accepted his, filling her. She leaned down and sucked his bottom lip between hers. This was a man she could envision spending her life with. She wasn't sure how she felt about children, but of him, Lysander Oshea… Verda Fairclough couldn't be more confident that he was the man for her.

She moved over him, her mouth mimicking her lower body, his hands guiding her motion, driving her momentum to a soaring height. Reaching for that peak of completeness while gasping for air. Her legs squeezed against his hips. Her inner walls tightened their hold on that powerful cock. She licked inside his mouth.

The pinnacle remained just beyond her grasp. She moved faster, chasing the unattainable until she traversed over the brink with a shrill cacophony Sander swallowed with his mouth. Her fingers sunk in his hair.

He didn't slow. Still fully encased within her, his hips rotated faster, harder. It seemed he couldn't go deep enough. And yet her body jerked with another swifter climax, jolting through her.

His low growl echoed through the chamber. The vibration penetrated to her soul. She landed hard against his chest, her arms cramping. "Verda."

"What?" she mumbled against him. "What was that?"

"That was our connection on a higher plane."

"Is there such a thing?"

"You tell me, love."

The emotion hit her with a bout of unforeseen tears. "I-I didn't know," she whispered.

He lifted her head and feathered her lips with the sweetest of kisses, thumbing the tears to oblivion.

A small smile filled her. "I can't imagine what possessed me to wait until I was nine and twenty for such bliss."

"Don't you, you saucy wench?" The quick flash of humor had her smiling wider against his lips. "I cannot fathom how you were not snapped up at your debut."

"I never had a debut. Papa… The cost…"

"Something for which I now owe him. You were waiting for me," he said.

Joy blossomed in her chest. Was it possible his feelings matched hers? "Remember when you asked me if you were my hero?" she asked him, her voice low and trembling at her sudden nerve.

His body stilled, every muscle touching her, taut. "Yes."

"You are indeed my hero."

His reaction was stark and immediate. Left no room for doubt that he must feel the same as his mouth crashed over hers again, hot, fierce, ravenous.

SANDER SHIFTED VERDA to his side and fought an overwhelming need to close his eyes and sleep. He was finding it especially difficult with her fingers drawing lazy circles on his torso.

"I believe I am fully energized," she said.

His groan was one of regret and resignation. "I am not a young man, love."

"Ah, you have aged. I hadn't realized I'd slept so long and, alas, soundly."

"Men require rejuvenation time."

Her fingers stopped their light whirling. "I don't understand."

"At the risk of unmanning myself…" He took her hand, kissed her fingertips, then moved her hand below to his now less-than-impressive staff.

With a sharp gasp—or was it a laugh?—she curled her palm over his softened form, and damn if it didn't stir with the contact. "*That* was inside me?"

His hand pressed down on hers. "Indeed, it was," he said with a staunchness that rivaled the Earl of Pender at his most pompous.

Breath from her gentle chuckle grazed his skin.

A contented silence pervaded and Sander closed his eyes to luxuriate in the tranquility of the moment, drifting on that higher plane. Though he'd been teasing her when he'd said it, he couldn't believe "higher plane" was the only phrase that fit the depths of his sentiment.

Sleep fringed his consciousness, prodding him to let go.

Beside him, Verda moved, laying her head on his shoulder. "How did Mr. Colbert die?" she asked quietly.

His eyes flicked open. "A rock."

The lips touching his skin frowned against him. "What are you saying? He tripped and hit his head on a rock?"

How was he supposed to answer such a question without ensuring her of more nightmares? "No…" He drew the word out.

"Someone hit him, then." She sat up. The jerkiness of her motion chased his sleepiness to the precipice alerting him of her sudden agitation. "Who?" Her voice wavered, sounding almost faint.

"We don't know." Sander had wracked his brain all day long to come up with an answer. If he hadn't witnessed the tick in his brother's cheek himself, he might have believed Damien capable of offing the man in a fit of temper. He'd even considered the fact that Colbert's death on Pender land of a plot to implicate Damien for the crime. But none of those scenarios resonated.

Sander sat up beside her and slipped an arm about her shoulders. "Enough of such a maudlin topic. I would much rather speak of our impending marriage."

"Marriage?" The mouse-like squeal had resurfaced and ascended to the rafters.

A most encouraging turn, he decided.

VERDA DREW IN a slow breath, while her heart pounded like heavy, uneven footfalls in an empty church. A second later, the erratic heartbeats leveled and annoyance set in. Sander's words were surely due entirely to his overly gentlemanly sense of duty. She swiftly detached herself from his hold. "That is completely unnecessary, sir." She almost made it from the bed.

Before one foot hit the floor, he had her by the wrist. "Oh, no, you don't, love. There will be no one-sided lines of repertoire followed by hasty escapes."

"Mr. Oshea," she said stiffly. "I am firmly on the shelf and not in need of your saving."

He tugged her wrist, flailing her to her back, then loomed over her. It was too dark to make out his expression. "I thought we agreed it was Sander," he growled.

"I don't feel like saying your name right now." Heavens. She sounded like a petulant child.

"So, my ruining you is not enough to entice you into wedded bliss, eh?"

A sudden sting burned her eyes. *No.*

"And if you're with child?"

She should shove him off her. But he was large, and warm, and curative for the life in which her father had imposed. Still, she wanted more. "You teasing me is not an enticement, sir."

He fell to her side and wrapped her in a cocoon of shelter. He let out a long sigh that warmed her temple. "Still, you'll marry me, won't you?"

"Yes, yes. I shall. But be warned, Mr. Oshea, I am not one who is swayed with sweet words and tenaciousness." The fabrication rolled primly from her lips. "But you win."

"Thank God. I was about to give up."

She burrowed in his side, smiling against the warmth of his skin. "Yes, I sensed it so," she whispered, letting his very tenderness seep into the depths of her soul.

CHAPTER TWENTY-SEVEN

WHEN VERDA WOKE the next morning, the chamber was decidedly, and sadly, void of Sander. Well, not completely empty.

Lizzie bustled about. Most notably gathering the variety of Verda's under garments over her arm. She laid them aside and picked up Verda's dress that lay over the back of the settee. "You should have woken me last night, miss—"

Blazing heat seared Verda's face at the activities that had transpired. She sent up a silent prayer for the miracle that Lizzie *hadn't* woken last night. "*What?*"

Lizzie shook out the gray wool, held it up, studying the front and frowning. "To help with your gown. What are all these snags in your frock? I vow, the buttons are decidedly loose…" Her voice trailed and her narrowed eyes surveyed the chamber that started in Verda's direction and ended at something hanging from the hearth.

Oh, dear.

The dress was thrown over Lizzie's arm as she marched to the dried cloth hanging there. It was too much.

Verda threw herself back, yanking the coverlets over her head.

"Is this *blood?*" Silence followed this denouncement, then, "Miss?" Her voice sounded much closer than it should have been.

With a defeated sigh, Verda peered over the edge of the bed-clothes. "Yes. All right? I'm nine and twenty. I will not be chastised by my maid."

"Chastised." Astonishment etched her elfin features. "I-I never—" Her mobcap wobbled precariously with the vigorous shake of her head. "I'm *envious*, miss."

Verda bolted upright. "Envious?"

"Oh, yes." Lizzie nodded and the mobcap slid over her eyes. She shoved it back. "It's been clear to me all along how besotted Mr. Oshea is."

"Besotted," Verda parroted. "I... He's... I..." He wasn't besotted. He'd as much said he would marry her because he'd ruined her. He was a second son and she a baron's daughter. To society, such a match was entirely acceptable. "Besotted?" she said again. Well, she had agreed to marry the man. He really was tenacious.

"He's most dashing."

Verda groaned, then shook her head. She threw back the covers and crawled from her nice, warm bed. Right now was not the time to ruminate on that particular issue. "Help me dress, then inform the children they are to break their fast in the morning room." Verda didn't doubt all conversation in the castle would revolve around Mr. Colbert's dead body. It was best to speak of it openly. "That goes for Olive, Miss Bash, and Master Julius as well," she added brashly." Speculation elevated fear, paranoia, and dark conjectures and she had every intention of nipping cabals before they could sprout wings and fly. "I want you there too." There was already too much rumination going about regarding 'the current haunting of Stonemare.' Hmm. What an enticing title for a horrid novel.

"Me?" Lizzie asked, startled.

"Yes. And, I'll wear the dark-green wool today."

Lizzie muttered something incoherent.

"Pardon?"

"I said, you'll never land the man with the wardrobe you packed."

"I can dress myself, you know. You could be removed to the

servants' quarters with the other maids." Verda hid a grin. "We are not attending a country house party. I'm here as a governess. The dress, please." She went to the escritoire and drafted a note to Mrs. Knagg informing her of Verda's unusual plans for breakfast that included all of the castle's occupants.

"Deliver this to Mrs. Knagg, Lizzie. If she balks, you may tell her, I am quite firm in my decision."

An hour later, Verda entered the morning room to a cacophony of chatter. With a sharp clap of her hands, the air cleared of excessive noise. "Thank you." She slipped off a shawl and draped it over the back of the chair between Noah holding Julius—and Lord Perlsea, who wore his brood like a well-worn cloak—then sat.

Miss Docia strode in with Olive on her heels and took the seat across... as elegantly as a queen, of course.

Fletcher and his counterpart were filling water glasses and setting them at each place at the table, which had been set for the entire household. A flock of nervous birds had taken residence in Verda's stomach. She couldn't imagine the earl's reaction when and if he appeared. She rather thought Sander might be highly amused by her outrageous edict.

A harried and worried Maura appeared, but the nursemaid caught sight of Julius and her lips compressed as if constraining a scold for Noah.

Verda narrowed her gaze, then turned to him. "Master Noah, did you happen to inform Miss Bash you'd absconded with Master Julius?"

"He was crying and *she* wasn't in the room." His sulky tone said much.

"Young sir," she said sharply. "Miss Bash is Master Julius's caretaker."

His mouth opened.

She held up her hand, palm out, staying any refute. "No, Master Noah. I cannot stress how important it is for Miss Bash to know where your brother is at all times. I'm not saying you can't take him with you. But henceforth, you will inform her when you do. Am I clear on this?"

The boy's bottom lip pulled out in his stubborn mulishness he'd affected as well as his brother had with his brooding.

"Master Noah?" she said again, knowing every eye in the dining chamber rested on the two of them. "Am. I. Clear?"

His eyes fell away first. "Yes, ma'am."

A collective breath seemed to release from those around her. She'd won this round.

Lizzie rushed in and went to stand by the windows next to Olive. Also there was Mrs. Knagg and the four house maids. Mr. Winfield and the only two footmen, Fletcher and—one other, she failed at remembering his name—moved to a set of doors that led to a terrace.

"Lizzie, you and Olive may take a seat at the table."

Unified gasps hit Verda from all sides.

"Please," she added.

Both lady's maids made their timid way over as if they feared vipers coiled in the chairs they took.

Sander strolled in. "Did I miss a notice?"

Lizzie's face turned as scarlet as Verda was certain hers had.

"You've a standing invitation," she told Sander, taking her serviette and placing it across her lap since using it to cover her face would be worse and infinitely more noticeable.

"Well, hell." Lord Pender stood in the door. "We're eating with the servants now?"

Olive and Lizzie started to rise and Verda pierced them with a frown. "You are today, my lord. Take your seats, everyone. You, as well, Lord Pender."

With an insolent glare, and to her surprise, he took his normal chair at the head of the table, at the opposite end from Sander, without further protest.

"Brava, Miss Fairclough," Sander said, where indeed, amusement glittered in his eyes. "Coffee and tea for all, Winfield, Mrs. Knagg. Er, milk for Julius," he corrected, then he aimed a knowing smile in her direction. "Now, what is the meeting of this intriguing rendezvous?"

Verda let out her own breath. "We all wish to know the particulars regarding Mr. Colbert."

Sander's grin disappeared. "There are children present, Miss Fairclough." He spoke slowly and deliberately, as if unsure she comprehended the language.

The grin reappeared—on the earl's face—and he lazed back against his chair. As if settling in for a show at Vauxhall.

That he didn't rub his hands together was a great surprise.

Docia's gaze flicked to Olive rising out of her chair, but Lizzie patted her hand and whispered something to her and she lowered back down. Docia's attention moved to Lord Pender. "What killed him?" Sometimes, Verda failed to appreciate the girl's forthrightness.

The earl looked as if he'd been whapped on the head.

Verda snuck a glance at Sander. His jaw appeared tight enough to crack.

"Perhaps that's a question for Sander, my dear," Lord Pender said. "He's the one with experience when it comes to dead bodies."

Annoyance nearly choked Verda. "That's enough, my lord. Mr. Oshea did not murder his father and I would appreciate you not teasing him as if that were the case."

Master Noah leaned forward until Julius's bum hit the tabletop. Glasses teetered and Verda quickly righted the two nearest ones. Three others, however, toppled.

She stole another glance—Sander's mouth hung open.

Noah patted Julius on the back. "Is that true, Uncle Sander? You murdered Grandfather?"

"That goes for you as well, Master Noah. It is certainly not true and I'll hear no more about it.," she said sharply.

He promptly sat back. "Yes, ma'am."

Lord Pender did not help matters. Not with that gleam of mirth he exuded. "Yes, ma'am."

Lord Perlsea's arms were crossed and his chin touched his chest. He had that brooding bit down, but Verda wanted to hug him. He raised his head and glared at his father. "I believe Father did the deed." They were the first words out of his mouth since learning of Mr. Colbert's unfortunate fate and being forced to remain home instead of accompanying the men to the parish constable, as he believed his due as heir apparent.

Thrilled as Verda was to hear him finally speak, she admonished him. "I said, that's enough, Lord Pender, please. I would have you reassure the children."

With a disdainful sniff, he said, "It's true. My brother did not murder our sire. He died of exposure on the moors."

Her gaze moved around the table. "There. You see?"

"It's why the moors are haunted," he added.

"Oh, for the sake of the dev—" Sander's impatience had gotten the better of him. "Damien, quit provoking my betrothed. Or we'll be here... for..."

The blaring silence was drowned out by the roaring in Verda's ears while every pair of eyes bore holes through her.

Perhaps *she* would be the one committing an unlawful death, she thought as the cacophony she'd effectively quelled earlier, exploded into a barrage of unanswerable demands for explanations.

"I knew it!" Noah wriggled in his chair and Julius's chubby legs kicked out, his toothless coos filling the air.

"Is it true?" Docia demanded, sounding as if it peeved her that her nuptials would not occur before Verda's.

Lord Pender's expression was something entirely different. "Interesting," he said in that sardonic way he had. "I thought the two of you already wed."

Shock held Verda immobile, an icy black fury edging her vision. How dare Sander make such an announcement without her... her... *Heavens.* She closed her eyes to garner her control, took in a deep breath through her nose, opened her eyes, and forced herself to meet his gaze head on.

The astonishment in his expression was enough to realize his words had not been intentional and softened her insides slightly.

She held up her hand to subdue the intemperate disorder. A minute later, the crowd quietened, where soon silence once more reigned. "I believe Mr. Oshea has spoken out of turn," she said, stunned she could sound so calm. "We are here to learn of past incidences as much as we are for present ones and I am not referring to Mr. Oshea's unexpected announcement." She turned a pointed look at the earl then shifted to Sander. "We should like an accounting of Mr. Colbert's circumstances. At least as much as you can tell us."

"As much as I disagree with relaying such information with children present, I will honor Miss Fairclough's request." Sander proceeded to relay the facts, much as he had the night before, with the earl throwing in an inappropriate remark here and there that Verda allowed to pass. The important thing to her was everyone having the same information.

The meal passed in a tolerable silence with utensils clinking against china and Julius being passed from person to person so Verda, Noah, Olive, Miss Bash, and even Lord Perlsea taking a turn, could eat in relative peace.

Eventually, Verda stood putting them out of their misery and announced lessons would begin in ten minutes amongst a series of relieved sighs and groans.

CHAPTER TWENTY-EIGHT

VERDA STRODE INTO the nursery with Julius's glass bottle and shivered. The chamber required more heat. Miss Bash was taking care of an infant, for heaven's sake. And where the devil was she?

The ancient and sparsely occupied frigid space boasted a worn rug that covered the entirety of the floor. At least it kept the cold from seeping through her thin slippers. A rocker, a rocking horse, a changing table, a crib, and a box filled with toys were the only items set about the huge room. A door near the hearth led to Miss Bash's bedchamber and Verda went over and tapped.

No answer. She peered inside, pleased to find Miss Bash had made her bed. There were no personal affects—photos, jewelry— to indicate the woman lived there. Just a hairbrush and a couple of hairpins on a sideboard next to the water basin and bowl for her daily ablutions.

Verda closed the door, went to the changing table, and set Julius's cylinder of milk atop. Her fingers brushed a note, sending it fluttering to the floor. Verda swooped it up with no intention of delving into Miss Bash's personal correspondence—and stopped.

She'd seen similar handwriting before.

When she and Sander had accompanied Docia home to pack for her stay at Stonemare. It was another childlike scrawl. But it was the words leaping from the missive that stung her skin with ice, driving all rational thought to the dregs.

Julius doesn't like you. He wants you to leave. You're a horrid nursemaid. I'll bet you never find us. Noah.

Noah. Where the devil would the little bugger hide? She stormed out of the chamber and started down the stairs, but a noise from somewhere stopped her. Forcing herself to take a breath, a little of her practical judgment asserted itself and she spun slowly, trying to determine if she was imagining things. No, it was the squeal of too rusty a hinge. Was he the next floor up? The stairs for that level were at the end of the hall. Blast that child. Noah had been warned time and again.

With an abrupt change of direction, she ran for the stairs.

The stairwell was unused in this portion of the castle. So said the cobwebs, waving her onward. Stone steps wound up through stone walls she could touch on either side of her and seemed to go forever.

She was going to pummel that boy! Not literally, but she would shake him until his head rattled from his body for putting an infant at such risk. Julius was a good baby but for his constant sniffles. He seemed his best when Noah had hold of him. That was what made this latest antic so outrageous.

The length of the ghastly, drafty stairwell equaled two normal ones. Verda was breathless by the time she stepped out on a narrow landing that turned out not to be a landing at all. A single door with a key in the keyhole that opened into a large storage attic. The only light came from a row of floor-to-ceiling windows. The light was laughable, however, due to the gloomy skies beyond.

Verda moved deeper into the attic through a path of dusty trunks. Unbearable cold reminded her she wore only her green, woolen frock. Unadorned with lace or even her threadbare shawl. It was still in the morning room hanging on the back of her chair, as the fire there had warmed her through. Cursing herself that she'd forgotten it. After breakfast, she'd traipsed down to the kitchens for Julius's cylinder of watered-down goat's milk. She maneuvered her way to the windows and gazed out.

Below, violent waves crashed against the foreboding rocks. Rocks that appeared more treacherous than those she'd witnessed on her daily treks along the cliff's path. She should have brought a candle.

The door creaked from behind her, wrenching her gaze. But that wasn't the worst part.

The key turned in the latch.

Panic shot through her, blinding her in her rush for the door. But she tripped, and fell, coming face to face with a bloodied— and dead—Maura Bash.

THE CHILDREN'S LESSONS should have been well underway and Sander charged into the library because he couldn't abstain another minute without seeing Verda. Without being in her presence, that was balm to a dissonance he hadn't even known plagued him. He just knew things were right when she was near.

Noah was placing Julius in his basket and looked up. "Good afternoon, Uncle Sander. Where's Miss Fairclough?"

Lucius, still apparently miffed, said nothing and didn't bother raising his eyes from the tome in his lap.

"I thought our lessons were to start at one," Docia said behind him.

"And yet it's one-fifteen." Noah sneered. "Where have *you* been hiding? Strategizing your next victim's demise?"

That statement jolted Lucius's attention. His eyes narrowed on his younger brother. "You know, it's said when someone hates one for no reason, it's really because they are secretly in love."

A laugh choked Sander in his attempt to swallow it back, noting the mottled red in Noah's furious features.

"That's to be expected," Docia said primly. She took her seat on the settee. "After all, marrying me would elevate his current stature." She smoothed her hands over her light-blue silk skirts. "At the appropriate age, of course."

Lucius snorted and dropped his eyes back to his book. "You're eleven," he muttered.

Through a huff of exasperation, Sander said. "You are children. There will be no further talk of marriage between any of you."

Docia gave him a wide-eyed stare that set his teeth on edge. "Why not? You and Miss Fairclough are to marry. I suppose it's perfectly understandable. You've been in her bedchamber. And you've referred to her as 'Verda.'" She punctuated the name with a single, sharp nod.

The hair on his neck raised. A grown man couldn't very well call out a child. A girl at that. Insolent though she may be.

The little termagant didn't miss a beat. "Of course, marriage to Miss Fairclough is acceptable, Mr. Oshea. She is a baron's daughter, after all."

Before Sander could wholeheartedly agree with her wisdom, Noah added his modest contribution to the discourse. "We've all been in Miss Fairclough's chamber at night." God bless his soul.

"Thank you for your insights and approval, Lady Docia. But I would marry her regardless," he confirmed, then he frowned. "When was the last time any of you saw Miss Fairclough?"

"She went to the kitchens after breakfast to retrieve the bottle for my Julius." He shrugged. "She probably took it to Miss Bash, not realizing I had him with me."

Lucius piped up. "That was over an hour ago."

"She may have gone for her walk." Docia shivered. "She doesn't much care if it's raining or not."

Thunder roared through Sander's head. "I thought I advised everyone to remain inside," he growled under his breath.

"You mean mandated," Lucius corrected him.

Noah nodded. "Commanded."

"Ordered," Docia added, as if believing she helped.

Sander's instincts rioted. Something was wrong. Very wrong.

Sending Noah or Lucius out to look for her was out of the question. With a deep breath that did nothing to steady his insides, he pointed to Lucius. "Go speak with Mrs. Knagg. See if Miss Fairclough did indeed head to the kitchens."

Sander looked at Noah, started to speak, but caught the edge of Julius's basket in his peripheral vision. "Stay with Julius." He turned to Docia. "Check the nursery. I'll look outside—"

Damien blocked the door. "Something wrong?"

"Verda is missing."

Damien waved out a hand. "Bah. She's likely using the chamber pot. Give the woman her privacy."

"You've lost your wits along with your memory," he said through a clenched jaw. "I shall check her chamber. You and Baldric cover the grounds. Against common sense, she does enjoy a walk on the path along the cliffs."

Lucius and Docia hurried out of the room.

"I'm sure she's fine," Damien told him.

"Go." Sander turned back to Noah and stared at his young innocent nephew, his heart pounding. After a short hesitation, he said, "If anyone comes in here, have them remain."

"W-What if my Julius wakes and needs to eat?" His bottom lip trembled.

"I suspect Mrs. Knagg will be here within minutes. You can have her return with another cylinder."

"All r-right. Do you think Miss Fairclough is…"

"She's fine," Sander assured him, blocking out any other option. "We just have to find her."

"Once you marry her, she won't get lost again."

"That is my exact plan, Noah."

Sander took the stairs two at a time, raced down the hall to the east wing, and burst into Verda's chamber—chamber pot or no.

Lizzie's hand flew to her chest. "Sir!"

"Where's your mistress?" he demanded.

"In the library. The children—"

"She's not there."

Lizzie frowned. "That's odd. She went to the kitchens to round up the infant's cylinder to take to Maura—"

Sander didn't wait. He tore out of her chamber for the stairs to the nursery, meeting Docia and Olive in the corridor.

"She's not there." Docia's eyes glistened with unshed tears. Her maid stood beside her, fear furrowing her forehead and wringing her hands. "I-I found this." She held out a note.

Sander snatched it from her fingers and quickly read it through.

Julius doesn't like you. He wants you to leave. You're a horrid nursemaid. I'll bet you never find us. Noah.

"Noah?" Sander raised a brow at Docia.

"I knew he was trouble. I couldn't possibly marry him after a stunt like this," she said, the tear tripping over her bottom lash and sliding down her cheek.

"Go down to the library and wait with the others." The note singed his fingertips. Without taking his eyes from the foolscap, he said, "Accompany your mistress, Olive. I'll be there shortly." His head came up. "Don't mention this to Noah. Pretend as if you didn't learn a thing."

"Why not? He's nothing but trouble," Docia said again. "You should sell him to the fencers in London, Mr. Oshea. He's a disgrace."

"Enough," he barked. "Just do as I say."

"Fine, but you mark my words." Docia flounced away with her fretful maid on her heels.

Sander listened to their footfalls on the stairs and returned his attention to the note. Noah hadn't written it. Sander would stake his life on the fact. Noah hadn't once referred to Julius without "my" as the prefix of his name. And the handwriting…

What had Docia said minutes before? That Sander had visited Verda's bedchamber. There had only been two nights. The first one was before Docia had even become a guest of Stonemare.

The second one: last night.

So, why the note?

It was true that Docia and Noah hated one another. More than was usual for neighbors. Their resentment bordered on irrational.

This note was beyond the pale. The obvious conclusion was Docia. The child was educated and eloquent. Savvy, and most devious. And, the cliffs? Was Docia, a child, so sinister to attempt pushing Verda over the cliffs?

Nothing else seemed to fit.

CHAPTER TWENTY-NINE

S HAKING, VERDA CAME to her knees. *This is not happening.* She put her hands on the floor to pull herself up and her left one slipped on blood. The smell hit her first and she gagged. She would *not* cast up her accounts. She was no longer eight years old. She was no longer without resources. She was a woman grown. She possessed common sense. Yet the urge to scream smothered her.

Maura was not her mother. She was a young woman who'd been attacked. She may not even be—

Right. She needed to take a breath, but if she smelled the blood again, it might be all over for both of them. She swiped her hand over her skirts and carefully came to her feet. Her whole body quaked, but she made it to the windows and laid her face against the cold pane, her hot hands flat. She drew back and breathed in. Deeply.

With that inhale came clarity. She edged her way back to Maura and touched her face. It was cold, but nothing like her mother's all those years ago. She took her hand. It was the same. Cold.

Verda used her own to warm her. "Maura? Can you hear me?" With little light, it was impossible to tell if the words had any effect. "Please, Mama." She blinked. "*Maura.* Do not die. I know I seem the most sensible woman ever, but I just couldn't bear it if anything happened."

Maura didn't move so much as a pinkie finger.

Distress raced rising panic. "Maura, *please.*" Verda patted her hand. Rigorously. "*Please.*" *Tears blinded her. She would never be warm again. The light. She needed light. But there were no candles. No fire...*

She'd fallen into her worst nightmare.

She ran for the window. Yanked on the heavy drapes. "I can't get it," she shrieked. "I can't get it."

Her sobs hiccupped. "Mama..."

Her words were broken. The latch was too hard... darkness closed in... she couldn't breathe...

"Oh..." The word was long, whispered, and drawn out.

Verda froze. She was... hearing things. But no, the fingers she held moved. "Maura?"

"Help me up."

"You mustn't strain yourself. Do you know what happened?"

Maura pulled her hand from Verda's and put it to her head. "No. A-Am I bleeding?"

"A little, I believe."

Now that Maura was conscious, Verda could see her panic for what it was. Much of her pragmatic self was returning, her brain not so full of mush.

"Why is it so dark?" Maura asked.

With a grim smile the young woman likely couldn't see, Verda indicated the windows, which she *also* couldn't see. "The windows are huge, but it's another murky day. So..." Her shoulder lifted. "No light."

"I think if you help me up, I can walk now."

"I'm relieved more than I can say to hear that. Unfortunately, we're locked in. I heard a key turn in the latch. If I had a candle, I might be able to find something with which to break open the door."

A short, companionable silence reigned over the attic. Shocking to Verda, considering her state of mind not ten minutes ago.

Maura broke the silence. "You're good with the children," she said, her tone thoughtful.

"Hmm. Not so much with Miss Docia," she countered. "Or Master Julius. He's sweet, though."

"I wouldn't worry much over Miss Docia. I don't think she likes herself very much."

The sentiment surprised Verda. She tilted her head. "I don't understand."

"Lady Chaston was quite active in the community when she was alive. She doted on Miss Eleanor and Miss Docia—"

"Miss Eleanor?"

"Miss Docia's older sister."

Verda frowned. "I didn't realize Docia had a sister. How old is she? Is she away at school?"

"Oh. No, she died last year. She would have been... mmm, sixteen this year, I believe. The same age as Olive."

"I had no notion," Verda murmured.

"The girls always accompanied their mother to the village. She was always telling Miss Docia how pretty she was and how, if she married well, she would one day be this grand lady. She was always calling her 'Lady Docia.' But that was years ago. Lady Chaston died of a contagion while his lordship was away in London. Of course, it seems he's always in London. Miss Docia was only five at the time. Truly? I always felt a little sorry for her. She really has no one left but her father, and as I said, he's never home."

It *was* sad. "Miss Eleanor contracted the contagion, then?"

"Oh, no. She fell and hit her head two years ago." Maura put a hand to her own head and spoke so matter-of-factly that it took Verda a minute for the words to sink in.

She drew in a sharp gasp. "Are you telling me she died from a... a *head injury*?"

"Yes, she—" Her abrupt stop showed she'd arrived at the same conclusion that hit Verda.

"I'm sensing a pattern here."

"You think Miss Docia... But she's only *eleven*."

"I don't know," Verda said slowly, "if it's Miss Docia, Olive, or the two of them working together." A vision of the two rushing in from outside flitted through her. Verda had difficulty in believing two young women able to fell one large man, albeit an aging one at that. "But… we need out of here."

But then recollections of her conversation with Docia cut Verda to her core. The bruise on her wrist. Had Docia hidden the actuality of how she'd sustained them?

Worse, and this was truly shattering, had Verda's skepticism inhibited Docia's candor of events? She swallowed hard. Her head ached with concern for a child who needed someone to listen and horrified she hadn't given the situation more careful consideration. The guilt was debilitating—

"I think I had a candle when I came up." Maura's words jarred her back to their bleak surroundings.

"Right, then. It must be somewhere near here." Verda went on her knees and squinted into the darkness, praying there weren't spiders. Her fingers brushed a candleholder. She was close. "Found it." The candle had rolled under a small table.

"Thank heavens."

"Blast. There's no way to light it." Verda had actually perfected the art of striking flint against steel, as she'd never intended to be trapped in a cold, dark room again in her life. But here she was trapped in an *attic*. "There must be something here somewhere." She came to her feet and worked her way toward the door. It was a tedious process with all the trunks, paintings stacked against the wall, chairs with broken legs, tables, a desk—"I've found an escritoire." She located the latch that lowered the writing surface and, using her fingertips, felt four drawers, two on either side of open compartments stacked with papers.

Starting with the first drawer, Verda went through each one with methodical precision. "We're in luck," she called out. Top-right drawer, she found flint and steel. Now, she just needed tinder and hope she didn't set the entire castle afire. Even more fortunate, she located a cracked basin and some old linen. She grabbed a stack of papers too then cleared a place near the windows.

Maura crawled her way nearby. "Is this safe?"

"Of course," Verda lied, then guilt set in. "Mostly. One moment." There must be something she could use as simple kindling. A couple of trunks offered promise, and she located one filled with old bedclothes. She grabbed one piece along and dropped it, still folded, into Maura's lap.

"I-I don't understand."

"In the event a fire does grow out of our control, you must smother the fire with that. Or have it handy for me to nab from you."

"All right." Her voice shook, but she seemed a sensible young woman. She had five siblings, after all, so Verda kept faith.

With honed practice, she ripped pieces of the foolscap into strips and dropped them atop the loosely gathered piece of linen. With the flint firmly in one hand and the steel in the other, she angled it toward her makeshift bowl of kindling and struck. A spark caught the paper on her first try. "It worked," she whispered. She dropped the flint and the piece of steel then leaned in and blew softly until it smoldered then flared to life. "Quick, hand me the candle."

Maura handed it over.

"And then there was light," she said with a satisfied grin. She glanced at Maura.

The nursemaid's eyes were wide as saucers. "How did you do that?"

"Practice." *And luck.* "Now." Verda took the folded bed cloth and smothered the fire. She took the candle and, holding it up, looked about. "This place is a shambles." She lowered it to the stack of papers but shifted it to the side and, leaning in, caught sight of a signature on the top page. She lifted the paper, studying it. It appeared to be some sort of Promissory Note. The signature showed a flourished, distinctive "P," as were the "e," the "n," even the "d." It was the last two letters that ended in a long, indistinguishable tail. "What year did the old earl expire?" she asked Maura, her eyes never leaving the paper.

"1810," Maura answered promptly.

Verda lowered the sheaf and met her questioning gaze. "You sound most certain."

Her gaze dropped to her hands and she fidgeted, then raised her eyes. "I told you I felt sorry for Miss Docia. She was five when her mother was taken from her." Maura shrugged. "It's nothing, really. I was five when the old earl was found on the moors. Our ages just sort of struck me as a connection."

The air left Verda's body in a deflated rush. "Of course," she said softly, believing her. Maura was very kind.

"Throughout the years, I would see Lady Chaston with Miss Eleanor and Miss Docia on Sundays at church. Lady Chaston was the kindest woman. She made a point of regularly visiting the needy. Her daughters' castoffs were always donated to raise funds for foundling homes.

"I remember Olive trying to cozy up to Miss Eleanor. They were the same age, you see. Miss Eleanor was much like her mother, too nice to give her the actual direct cut. Eventually, I believe Lady Chaston felt sorry for Olive and that's how she secured the post as the young misses' lady's maid."

The deluge of information overwhelmed Verda and had her pinching the bridge of her nose.

A frown creased the young woman's forehead. "Did you find something?"

Verda quickly dropped her hand and stared at the paper again. "No. Nothing. This is dated 1811." But the hair at her nape raised. She folded the paper and stuffed it in her pocket.

A single pound hit against the door, startling Verda. Her head flew up, but her body stilled. The latch rattled.

Dear heavens. The murderer returned. They were going to rot in this dust-filled, cobwebbed hovel. "Stay down," she whispered.

THE SKELETON KEY was in the door and Sander's hope sagged. It had been lodged in the keyhole for as long as he could remember. The attic was literally the only place no one had thought to search. The frozen air clung to the tower. There was a reason no one ever came here. Frustration hit him with a force he transferred to his fist. "Damn." Still, he turned the key and pushed the latch just to be sure.

The first thing that hit him was the acrid stench of charred fabric—the second thing was the small shadow that danced on the ceiling. Every muscle was strung taut as a bow. "Verda?"

Her head raised and the candle's flame gave her face a cadaverous appearance. "Oh, Sander, thank heavens. We're here."

We're. "Thank God," he breathed.

"Maura and I. Someone locked us in."

Sander lifted his own candle. The path to the windows was narrow. He set the holder on an open escritoire and took the path, shoving furniture, trunks, and boxes out of the way with undiluted fury.

"Careful, Sander. Maura was knocked on the head, if you can believe it."

He went down on one knee, lifted Verda's chin, and kissed her full on the lips—hang any delicate constitution of the nursemaid. He pulled back, but Verda's lips clung to his. He glanced at Maura. Blood matted her hair. "What happened?"

The nursemaid shook her head. Carefully, he noted.

"She can't remember." Verda squeezed the girl's hand. "I took Julius's bottle of milk to her, but she wasn't there. I was convinced that she'd gone after Noah. I reached the stairs and I heard something from above. I came in and before I realized it, someone was closing the door and locking it." She shivered.

"Thank God you had a candle," he breathed. After that harrowing tale she'd relayed the night before—

"She didn't," Maura said in a rush of pride. "She used flint and steel. The sparks caught on the first try. Isn't that right, miss?"

"Perhaps we can save that conversation for a later time,"

Verda said.

"Oh, we definitely will." Sander assisted Maura to her feet, then held out his hand to Verda. He'd never felt so warm and relieved at the same time. He took her candle and guided the women through the haphazard path. Near the door, he handed Verda the other candle from the escritoire. It didn't take much urging from him for Verda and Maura to escape the biting cold of the attic.

After relocking the door, he pocketed the key for safer keeping.

"We need to retreat to the library," Sander said.

"We must find Julius. He's missing." Verda's frantic tone banded his chest. He reached for her hand and squeezed.

"No, he's with Noah. Come, everyone is waiting."

On the floor below, Maura stopped in front of the nursery's door. "I-I have to retrieve the baby's glass of milk."

Sander nodded and she disappeared inside, leaving him with Verda. The effort it took to restrain himself from taking her in his arms was painful.

She glanced at the door, then to him. "Sander," she whispered. "There's something I—"

"I'm ready." Maura stood in the arch and Sander had never heard her return.

He glanced at Verda, curiosity licking at him. "Of course, Maura. Shall we?" He led the way down to the ground floor and ushered Verda and the nursemaid inside.

Damien stood at the hearth, his lips in a compressed line, his eyes more alert than Sander had witnessed in years. Lucius stood at the windows, peering out, and Noah was pacing with his hands squeezing in and out of fists, darting looks at Docia, and her maid, Olive, who was holding Julius and sitting near the door.

"Shall I take the babe?" Maura asked Olive.

Olive smiled. "Oh, but he's settled in so nicely."

Maura held up the cylinder. "I have his milk, if you need it."

Olive took the glass. "Oh, yes. Thank you."

Maura followed Verda to the settee, but Verda didn't sit. She pulled a piece of paper from her pocket and offered it to Damien. "Is this familiar to you, Lord Pender?"

Snatching it from her fingers, he moved to the scarred table for light and quickly read. His face jerked up, blotched with fury. "Where did you get this?"

"The attic where someone locked me in."

Sander strode to his brother and took it from him and also read it through. "I recognize this name. Tamera Townsend. She was our mother's maid here some fifteen or twenty years ago."

"Seventeen," Damien bit out through clenched teeth.

"If I recall correctly, she left the castle under a shroud of..." He dropped his head and reread. "This is a promissory note." The vague details trickled in. "She was with child..."

"She lived in the village until her death," Maura said softly. "She was quite nice, really, if somewhat reclusive. Especially after Olive went to work at Chaston Manor as the Misses Eleanor and Docia's maid."

"Olive?" Sander's own jaw was near to shattering. "I take it you fathered..." He faltered. "But what has that to do with—"

A gasp sounded from behind, but he couldn't tear his eyes away from the unfolding scene before him.

Verda laid her hand on his arm. "Lord Pender, admittedly I'm overstepping here. However, I feel it incumbent to speak my mind."

"It has not stopped you before, Miss Fairclough," he said with sardonic disdain. "Don't mind my delicate feelings, ma'am. Feel free to proceed."

"Frankly, sir, your reputation—" She stopped and her gaze strayed to Lord Perlsea, Noah, and Docia, all watching her with an intensity that jolted Sander with a shock of lightning. "How old were you, sir?"

Sander waved the children to the other side of the room with a stern glance and turned back.

Damien's expression tightened.

"We were sixteen and seventeen," Sander growled out.

Verda's hands flattened on the table he sat behind and she leaned forward. In a lowered voice, she did not hold back. "Your reputation leaves much to be desired, my lord, and while that is neither here nor there, you must ask yourself if that document you are holding could have anything to do with the fact that Maura and I were locked in a dark attic without heat or light. More importantly, sir, Olive is sixteen."

The words sunk into Sander like the serrated edge of a dagger. Crestfallen, his chin hit his chest. "Dear God, Damien," he breathed. He turned to Verda. "You believe Olive is Tamara Townsend's illegitimate child?"

"I-I don't know," she admitted, then she shook her head before lifting her eyes to his. "There are… just little things that strike me. She has yours and"—her gaze flashed to Damien and back, cleared her throat—"Lord Pender's dark hair and gray eyes."

"Did Olive lock you in the attic?"

"Someone did." Slowly, Verda straightened, as if coming out of a trance. Turning about and seeming to survey the curious faces watching her every move, her gaze stopped near the open door. Her body went rigid as a slab of marble. "Where are Olive and Miss Docia?"

Noah's gaze flew to the empty chairs there. "She stole my Julius." His voice sent ice through Sander's veins as Noah dashed from the library.

Verda was the next to react, racing for the door on his heels.

Sander, with Damien at his side, rushed after them.

Noah and Docia gripped Olive's dress like a lifeline. "We've got her, Father," Noah said.

Sander strode to Olive. "I'll take the child, my dear," he said gently.

With a soul-breaking cry, she relinquished Julius to his possession. She turned a furious glare on Lord Pender. "You," she screamed, throwing the glass cylinder at him. It struck his chest then hit the floor, shattering, filling the foyer with its sweet and subtle grassy aroma. "This is all *your* fault." Her screech shook the candle-heavy chandelier over their heads.

A startled Julius released his own shrill cries.

Noah let go of Olive and came to Sander. "I'll take him now, sir."

Sander nodded, handing the baby off and took Olive's arm in a firm grip. "Docia, please accompany Noah to the library and wait there."

Without argument, the children vanished.

Verda and Lucius stood off to the side, eyes wide and horror-filled.

"You as well, Lucius. This is a matter for your Father and me. Perhaps we should take this conversation to the study," Sander suggested. "Miss Fairclough?"

"I shall accompany you." There would be no convincing her otherwise. And why should he? She would soon be mistress of his home and life.

With a sharp incline of his head, he glanced at his brother.

But Damien's expression was difficult to discern. He spun on a booted heel and marched down the hall, leaving Sander to take charge of Olive and follow.

Damien didn't hesitate in his inquisition after slamming the door behind the small ensemble. He turned on Olive. "Why did you kill Cracked?"

The question caught Sander by surprise. He let go of Olive and stood with his back against the door and his arms folded over his chest.

"He accused me of being a... a whore." Tears streaked down Olive's cheeks.

Upon closer examination, Sander could detect the faint resemblance to the Oshea line Verda had so cleverly discerned—primarily, it was her coloring, as she had observed. The dark hair, the gray eyes. It was the glittering disdain that hit him with stunning revelation.

"He thought I was my mother. He wouldn't shut up about it. Kept saying it over and over, until I picked up the rock and *shut* him up." Her chest heaved with harsh breaths.

The intensity of Damien's gray eyes churned with molten steel. He stalked to Olive and with one hand, gripped her chin. "There have been too many *accidents* of late," he said in a voice that matched his eyes. "What happened to Miss Eleanor, Olive? Did she truly trip down the stairs in Chaston House? Or did you push her?"

Verda's gasp echoed against the silk-covered walls.

But Olive didn't appear to hear. "All your other children live under your care. But not me. Why not me?" Her voice escalated with each uttered sentence. "It's unfair."

Because you are an illegitimate child of the great Lord Pender. The truth hurt Sander's insides. His brother's actions through the years had caught up with him. It was a tragic situation he wished more than anything from which he could extract everyone.

"And Miss Docia?" Verda said softly.

"She's nothing but a manipulating little princess no one likes."

"Did you mistreat her, Olive? Did you hit her? Mark her with bruises?"

"I hate her. I hate her. I hate her…" Her voice trailed off in a whimper.

"Calm down," Damien barked without an ounce of sympathy. He looked at Sander. "What am I supposed to do with her? She's too dangerous to set free."

"You could marry her off," Sander suggested, a facetious statement at best. "But she might dispose of the unsuspecting man."

"Sander, please," Verda interjected. "Such remarks do nothing to resolve the issue. What of one of your other properties, my lord?" she directed to Damien.

"An excellent point." Damien couldn't seem to take his eyes off Olive. Perhaps he was finally coming to terms with how his behavior affected those around him. "I'll ship her to Perlsea Keep. Upton runs a tight household." He glared at Olive.

Someone had to right the wayward path in which this conversation had veered. "Absolutely not. Need I remind you, this isn't some bauble she's lifted from an unsuspecting victim. She murdered a man and possibly a mistress she served."

"Right." Damien let out a long, shuddering sigh. "Then what do you propose, old wise one?"

Sander moved from the door and opened it. "Winfield," he barked.

The stately man appeared instantaneously as Sander knew he would. "Tell Baldric to fetch Broyle."

"Right away, sir."

"The constable?" Olive's voice was a squeal that nearly burst Sander's eardrums.

Damien gathered his verve. "We've no option, my dear bastard child. You shall likely only be transported." He seemed to age ten years past his current thirty-four and slammed his hand on the desk. "The alternative is being strung up by your scrawny, little neck."

Sander straightened and narrowed his eyes on her. "You wrote the note indicating Noah had hidden with Julius?"

Olive lifted her pointed chin and jutted it out. "What of it?"

"So, you lured Maura, then Miss Fairclough to the attics and locked them in?"

Large tears pooled in violent, stormy eyes. Her lips remained stubbornly closed.

"What was the purpose behind the false Chaston's note?" Verda asked her.

The girl seemed to deflate before his eyes. "He was walking out the door without a word."

"A word to whom? You? His daughter?"

Her lips tightened and sent a shot of apprehension through Sander. Chaston and Olive? It wasn't unheard of, but the thought sickened him.

"But why?" Verda whispered. "What purpose could you have for such antics?"

Sander took Verda's hand and squeezed gently. Meeting her sudden gaze, he gave his head a single shake.

Her open mouth snapped shut.

He glanced at Damien. The thoughtful look on his face was on Olive. A second later when comprehension dawned, he passed a hand over his face. He met Sander's eyes with a helplessness that took him back to their childhood days. Back when Sander had sheltered him from their father's unholy wrath.

Sander released Vera's hand and went to Olive. "Come, my dear. Let's find you suitable accommodations for your wait." The temptation to dole out his own sense of justice for locking the love of his life in the attic deserted him in a flood of pity.

CHAPTER THIRTY

THE LONG DAY had taken its toll. Sander entered Verda's bedchamber without so much as a knock. He needed to hold her. He needed to touch her. She was the strongest person he'd ever known.

She was sitting before the hearth, running her fingers through the dark fire of her hair. "Mr. Oshea—"

He stormed to her, yanked her to her feet, and took her mouth. Harshly, completely. Once she'd melted against him, he broke away. "*Never* call me that again."

"Sander?" she breathed.

The hair raised on his skin. He fell to one knee, tightening his hand on hers. "I love you, Verda. We shall soon be man and wife. We leave for Scotland in the morning and be home by afternoon."

She brought his hand to her lips. "I love you too." Her brilliant emerald gaze never wavered from his. "But—"

He tugged her to her knees with his hands secured on her upper arms, their chests nearly touching. "No buts." He slid his mouth over hers in a kiss that promised sunrise and sunset with all the colors that brightened his world no matter the weather in the wilds of the winter Northumberland.

She tasted of spun sugar sweetness, her lips plump and molding to his, giving what he demanded, and demanding from him in return.

"I'm never letting you go." He licked the space where her

shoulder curved into her neck. Took great satisfaction in her rapid breaths stirring the hair over his ear. "Never."

"You say that quite often," she whispered.

He smiled against her skin. "What?"

"Never."

"Yet I'm a man of my word." He came to his feet then pulled her to hers. With deft fingers, he dispelled with her wrapper. Untied her virginal white gown at the neck. "This is no longer needed."

She raised her arms and he eased it over her head. Dropping back to his knees, he buried his face in her abdomen and licked her stomach. The spicy aroma of sex filled his nostrils, overpowering the soft, powdery violet scent that was all her. He urged her legs apart and touched the apex with his tongue. Licked his way to heaven until her knees shook and threatened to give way.

With a quick spin, he had her on the settee and his tongue delving deep inside her. He suckled and bit and tasted. She writhed beneath his ministrations until he thought he would come in his breeches. It was her that flew apart, whispering his name over and over. And not one "Mr. Oshea."

He stood and tore off his waistcoat and his lawn shirt, then kicked off his boots and moved his hand to the placket—

Her fingers stayed him. "Let me." The husky tonality was almost enough to do him in, but he lowered his hands to the fire of her hair.

She may not have been as adept as him, but he resisted tearing at the buttons, sucking in his stomach to make things easier for her. Cool fingers touched the blazing heat of his skin as she pushed his trousers over his hips. He wore no short pants. It would be skin against skin in mere seconds—

Hot breath feathered his cock and he nearly lost all control. The damp touch of her tongue traced his length and all thought crashed from him like the so-prevalent waves against the rocks. He had to stop her or…

"I can't," he moaned.

She froze. "Can't?"

Sander pulled her up. He turned and fell on the settee with her hands in his. "Put your knees on either side of me. Hurry. I can't wait."

She didn't argue.

He positioned himself for her. "Lower on me."

Her hands moved to his shoulders, and her eyes were cast down to where their bodies were joining, her hair hiding her face. The tight sheath of her swallowed him and he moaned again. "I can't wait," he said again. He surged up until she gasped. "Are you all right?"

"Yes."

"Thank God." He pumped until she exploded and pulsed and suctioned against the fire branding rod his cock until he too flew over into the abyss that was her.

This love, now, was his life. *She* was his life.

Verda fell against his chest, the perfect synchronization of their breath, the only sound but the crackling fire that stretched and blanketed Sander with something deep and indefinable.

She was the first to break the silence. "About Scotland..."

THE ROAD INTO Scotland jarred Sander's brain nearly from his head. This wasn't exactly what he'd had in mind for his intimate marriage to Verda—him sitting atop the crowded barouche with Dermid, and Fletcher, the cold wind biting through his greatcoat. But truly? He knew he would never be cold again, not with Verda at his side, in his bed, in his life.

The trap door banged and he opened it.

Noah's furrowed brows peered from the dark. "Are we there yet, Uncle Sander? My Julius is quite tired of riding."

"You should have thought of that before organizing the entire family in accompanying me to my wedding," Sander told him. In truth? Sander wouldn't have it any other way. The only dark spot on his heart was the absence of Damien. "We'll be there within the hour, son."

The door shut with a clap. Sander threw off the melancholy thought of his troubled brother. A small burst of unadulterated laughter erupted from him. Verda would soon be his before God and family.

Fletcher turned a wary look on him. "Sir?"

Sander clapped him on the back. "Don't you realize, Fletcher? This is the first adventure of my new life." He embraced the cold air with zeal. With hope. With love.

Thirty minutes later, Sander stood at the altar of the small chapel in Paxton with Verda's hand clasped in his. Lucius, Noah, and Julius stood at his side with Docia and Maura at Verda's.

The vicar was a hearty Scot with a thick head of light-red hair, bushy beard, and twinkling, blue eyes. "You may kiss your bride."

"Finally," Sander breathed.

"Finally," Verda murmured.

Sander lowered his head to Verda's raised lips. This was forever.

⸭━━━◆◆◆━━━⸭

EPILOGUE

Three years later

STONEMARE WAS IN an uproar. The August rains saturated the moors. The wedding breakfast for Fletcher Grahame and Maura, er, Mrs. Fletcher Grahame, now, was a noisy and joyous affair. Lucius and Noah had arrived from school and were home for a few weeks before their scheduled return.

Lord Pender—Damien—strode in on their heels, shocking the entire household, not having been seen since escorting Olive Townsend to a quiet lunatic asylum located near Colchester by the name of Tranquil Waters some three years past.

Lucius's brooding had mellowed, but Verda sensed it beneath the surface. He was quite sensitive, but of course, telling him such would never do.

Noah was a joy. It was clear how much he'd missed Julius, but Julius was his own little terror. Never slowing until he dropped where he stood for Maura, Verda, or Sander to deliver him to his bedchamber.

Thirteen-year-old Noah stood stoically before her, eyes glistening with a suspicious sheen. "He acts as if he hates me."

"He doesn't hate you, darling. I believe he's growing independent and that's a good thing. Someday, he'll learn what brilliant care you took of him and he'll love you all the more for it."

"Are *you* having a baby?" he asked.

Heat infused her face and she fidgeted with her skirts, deciding on the best course of action in which to reply. Honesty usually served her purposes. She leaned in and took his hand. "Yes, but I've yet to tell Sander."

"Why not?" His brows drew together as he tilted his head and looked her straight in the eye. "I shouldn't return to school. You may need my assistance. I'm experienced, you know."

She smiled then tugged him into a hug. "You are indeed experienced." She pulled back and leveled a stern gaze on him. "But your education is of great importance and I will absolutely insist you return to school. As for your uncle… I only just learned myself."

The door to the library opened and Sander entered. The cloud of contentment that served as his private umbrella enveloped the room. Verda's heart overflowed with emotion.

"Oh, hello, Uncle Sander. Congratulations on your upcoming child," Noah said.

Verda gasped.

Sander stilled. "Pardon?"

"Aunt Verda just told me." He strode to the door. "I'd best check on my Julius. He may hate me, but I'm still his guardian angel, whether he likes it or not." The door slammed behind him.

Sander prowled across the chamber like a ferocious tiger. "You're having my child?"

She donned her most prim and reserved exterior. "It would seem so, Mr. Osh—"

"That's it!" In a blink, she was on her back and his mouth covered hers. The sentiments overflowing from her spilled through him back to her. His touch, his love, his devotion.

There was no time for more intense ardor because the door flew back and the family poured in. But the mood was dark and frightening.

Verda struggled to sitting and quickly straightened her bright-blue frock. "What's wrong?" she demanded.

"My Julius is missing," Noah choked out.

"Missing?"

"I-I think he went outside," Docia said.

"But how is that possible—" Verda started.

Lord Pender stood in the arch. "I'll find him, the little bugger." He spun away and the vestibule door opened then shut.

A heavy silence weighed the atmosphere.

But Maura appeared holding the little cherub, an angel with a jam-covered face. His head of dark hair lay on her shoulder. "The little miscreant had escaped to the kitchens and was stuffing his face with a jam-filled tart.

Noah marched over to Julius and poked a finger on his little pug nose. "You are a bad, bad boy, scaring the family half out of their wits like that."

Julius lifted his head with that impish grin on his oh-so adorable face that would likely save his future fate in less-than-favorable ways, his azure eyes lowing in an innocent blink. He raised his arms out for his brother, who snatched him from Maura and hugged him close then refused to let him down for the rest of the night.

No one appeared to notice that Lord Pender hadn't returned. But Verda had.

Sander sauntered up from behind and wrapped his arm around her waist. "Come, love, let's go to bed."

She leaned her head back, on his shoulder, pushing thoughts of her troublesome brother-in-law to the recesses of her mind. It wasn't like the flighty lord wouldn't appear out of the blue now and again without word.

She pressed her hands atop Sander's on her abdomen. This was her—*their*—hers and her darling husband's future.

Yes. Life was *wonderful*.

About the Author

Kathy L Wheeler writes historical and contemporary romance and has hit the Amazon Best Seller list several times over. In the face of danger, her heroines save themselves, their heroes just need to be there to catch them… after the fact.

Her many joys include the NFL, Musical Theater, travel (for example: she once spent twenty-one days going from Oklahoma City to San Francisco and back through Utah to Colorado. When her husband called to ask if she was coming home anytime soon, she then headed back home), and … karaoke.

Main sources of inspiration? Yes, well, they come mostly from an over-active imagination. She currently resides in the Pacific Northwest with her musically talented husband, Al, and their adorable dog, Angel who lives up to her name—*mostly*.

kathylwheeler.com

facebook.com/kathylwheeler

Instagram.com/kathylwheeler

TikTok.com/@kathylwheeler

YouTube.com/@kathylwheeler-author

www.ingramcontent.com/pod-product-compliance
Lightning Source LLC
Chambersburg PA
CBHW060448310726
48977CB00001B/358